STIRRING HER COWBOY

KATHY FAWCETT

CHAPTER 1

"Colton! Just the man I was looking for."

Colton West was swaggering through the ranch kitchen with his youthful, ruddy good looks, when he was stopped by his sister-in-law, Kat. He, of course, would do anything she asked. Although everyone knew there was a new girl in his life, one who had the handsome young cowboy wrapped around her little finger.

And she was sitting at his feet—hitting his sock with a pink plastic rattle.

"What do you need, Kat?" He dropped down to roll a ball to his niece, Willow. She was on the floor, surrounded by toys—many of them gifts from Colton himself, who just "happened" to find cute little things for her to grab and chew while in his travels.

The baby laughed when she saw her uncle, and kicked her feet with excitement, threatening to topple over backwards. Lightning quick, Colton placed a steadying hand on Willow's back until she was sitting straight again.

"There you go little lady," he said to the baby.

Kat smiled down at the cozy pair, though they paid her no mind. She almost forgot what she needed, then remembered.

"The renovations in the cook house are nearly finished," Kat said, "except for the shower head. It arrived after the contractor left, but I need it installed ASAP."

Colton remembered that the new ranch cook, someone named Lou, was arriving that day.

"Yeah, I can go install that," Colton said, rolling the ball again to the laughing baby.

"You're a life saver, Colton," Kat said, handing him the box. He kissed the baby on the top of her head, and stood waiting until she waved *buh-bye* with her chubby hand.

"Buh bye, buh bye," Colton said to a mesmerized Willow.

"Buh bye," Kat said to Colton, by way of speeding up his exit.

"All right, I'm going," he said with a smile, reluctantly leaving the kitchen—and his niece.

Minutes later Colton drove up to the cook house, which had been renovated from bow to stern. Leaving his dusty boots outside, Colton walked in and took a peek at the rooms.

The old kitchen now had pristine sub-zero appliances. A shiny stainless-steel work top stood in the center for food prep, complete with stools for guests.

The living room boasted new hickory floors and freshly painted walls in a dove gray. The old furnishings had been donated to a charity store, and new sofas and chairs took their place in trendy terra cotta tones with lime green accents. No charity shop had wanted the ratty old brown recliner, so a few weeks ago it was tossed on the camp cook's farewell bonfire.

When an early snowstorm hit West Gorge the previous September, Justice claimed it was his last winter—and he meant it. He stayed at the ranch through May. As soon as he left for sunny days in Florida, the contractor arrived and got to work.

Here it was, nearly July, and his replacement was due any minute.

Colton popped his head into the bedrooms to see fresh linens on new mattresses and sleek headboards. To the rancher, it looked like an upscale hotel instead of the old rugged "cabin" the cook had called home for thirty years.

He made his way into the bathroom with the walk-in shower, and whistled.

"I hope this *Lou* guy appreciates all this," he said out loud. Everything that was brown had been replaced with white subway tiles and shining marble. The shower itself was white, with a half wall made from glass brick. The effect was sunny and light. And maybe a bit more *feminine* than a grizzled old ranch cook would appreciate, Colton thought but wouldn't say.

He didn't want to get in Kat's business when it came to design.

Colton, in his stocking feet, stood inside the shower area to affix the new shower head. All too quickly, he realized the water was still turned on. Without warning, the spray from the open spout shot at him with a mighty SPLOOSH, soaking every layer of his clothes down to his skin.

"*Awww* darnit!" Colton exclaimed loudly, backing away from the forceful spray.

Looking down, he knew he was too wet to air dry. He quickly stripped off every stitch and walked the wet pile to the laundry room, tossing everything in the new front-load dryer.

"Good thing I'm alone in the house," Colton said under his breath as he made his way back to finish the installation.

He turned the water on again, and took his time regulating the settings. He was in his altogether, so didn't mind getting wet. It felt good. Standing under the flow, he tightened all the bolts, and stepped back to admire his handiwork.

Seeing that Kat had thoughtfully put soap in the shower, Colton took advantage of the moment and lathered up. Might as well, he thought. The day had been warm, and his clothes would need more time to dry, anyway.

"Sorry dude," Colton said out loud in the empty room as he scrubbed and rubbed, "you won't be the first guy to christen this luxury spa, Lou."

Humming a tune, Colton enjoyed the new surroundings as he let the warm water wash away the dust of his workday. He still helped out at the ranch when Gunnar needed, especially during the winter months when construction was halted. But heading up the development of West Gorge Woods was miles ahead more satisfying to Colton than being a rancher.

He felt proud of having a hand in Pike and Paislee's massive farmhouse, recently completed. It turned out beautifully, as had their outbuildings and studio. The white house with black framed windows and metal roof was strikingly modern, yet warm and inviting.

Inside, the design featured a complex pattern of angled walls and canned spotlights to accommodate Paislee and Pike's shared love of fine art.

It wasn't long before others wanted to move into the new community; they now had ten new homes going up. And two restaurants were under contract.

If only those restaurants were already open, Colton thought with stomach rumbling, he'd be happy.

He scrubbed his hair and the back of his neck, then ran his hands roughly over his bristled face. His stubbled beard would shine from the underlying tan, he knew. He had been outdoors most of the Wyoming spring and summer.

Gunnar West was the image of their father, Ridge, with some of their mother's height thrown in the mix. Pike West was the mirror image of their departed mother, Randi; tall and lean. And Colton—well, he knew he was somewhere in the middle. He got his stockiness from Ridge—the kind of physique that had made him a natural quarterback on the West Gorge High football team his senior year.

But like the others, he also inherited some of his mother's stature. And thanks to her, his mouse-brown hair quickly bleached into blonde with the first summer rays.

His stomach rumbled as he rinsed the soap off, making Colton grateful Kat hired a new cook. Justice would be a tough act to follow, but the young man looked forward to eating robust meals again. Kat's cooking kept them alive on the days she was willing. On other days, they either took a drive to Cindy's Diner or Red's Rib Shack, or fended for themselves.

"You can fry an egg, surely," Kat had told Colton on more than one occasion. Other days, Willow's mashed bananas and oatmeal had started to look good to the hungry young cowboy.

Turning the shower off, Colton stood still and let the water drip off him. He had forgotten to locate a towel before lathering up, so extended the drip-dry process. Noises coming from the kitchen caught his attention.

Lou must be bringing in some boxes, Colton thought.

Standing in the steam, he thought he could wait until he heard the cook house door open again, meaning Lou was back outside—then he'd dash through the house towards his clothes.

Before he could exit, unrinsed lather dripped into his eyes. He squeezed them shut against the stinging pain.

"Ahhh!" he shouted in surprise and agony.

"You okay?" It was a woman's voice, coming from the shower doorway he was about to walk through. Directly in front of him.

"Yeah, just some soap in my..." Colton started to say, and then froze.

CHAPTER 2

*H*is position couldn't have been more vulnerable and he knew it—soaking wet and standing in a cloud of steam, with his clothes clear on the other side of the house.

Blinking hard, Colton dared to open his eyes and was surprised to come face to face with a towel, being offered to him by a delicate and manicured hand. The arm and the rest of his rescuer was around the corner, outside of the shower doorway. Colton quickly wrapped the towel around his waist—it wouldn't make the full circuit, but it got the job done. Then he carefully stepped out of the shower to see a person standing before him in the fog.

She was young, with jet-black hair, and wore navy cat-eye glasses. Thankfully, the lenses were steamed up.

"Howdy," she greeted him.

Confused, but grateful for the towel, Colton was speechless at first.

"Howdy," Colton said eventually, as cool and casually as he could, considering his embarrassment. He fought the instinct to run, because he would have bowled her over.

The woman raised her eyebrows, but couldn't contain a smile as she removed her glasses to see him more clearly. She held his gaze with the most beautiful almond shaped eyes Colton had ever seen.

"Maybe you're my new *sous chef*," she said, with great humor in her eyes. "I guess I don't need to ask you to wash your hands."

Colton held the towel even tighter, and wondered in great agony who this woman was.

"Sorry, I was... fixing the shower," he stammered, "for Lou... the new ranch cook."

She smiled again at Colton.

"Thanks for doing that, I'm Liu," she said. "Liu Chen."

"*You're* the new cook?" Colton said in surprise.

"I prefer *chef*," Liu answered.

And at that, she pivoted and left the vapors of the bath area. But not before calling over her shoulder, "get your clothes on, cowboy. I could use some help."

He watched her slender body walk away. She was wearing skinny jeans and her feet were bare. Her yellow tee shirt was snug, and had an illustration of sushi, with the words: "This is how I roll."

Liu wasn't wearing much jewelry, just a sterling silver bracelet and a chunky wrist watch with a striped nylon band. The kind fighter pilots wore.

Colton felt the towel slipping. Before the young woman could turn towards him again, he dashed into the laundry room and shut the door. There, he frantically started putting on his clothes, hot from the dryer.

"Ow ow *ow*," he said, rushing the process.

She was Liu, Colton realized, not *Lou.*

And she was a *she.* Why hadn't Kat made that clear? But why had he *assumed*—that would be Kat's defense, if she were to have any at all.

Dang, Liu was pretty, though. He could get used to seeing her face at the ranch. It was only fair—she had gotten more than a good look at him.

Minutes later, Colton sheepishly walked back into the kitchen, fully dressed. Liu was standing behind the island with a cutting board in front of her. She wore a private smile on her face, and looked perfectly at home already, surrounded by boxes and grocery bags overflowing with the stems and greens of fresh fruits and vegetables.

"Sit," she commanded.

She was pointing to one of the island stools with the tip of her knife.

"I'm Colton," he said as he lightly perched on a stool. "Colton West."

"Nice to meet you Colton," she said in a clear, confident voice. "You look hungry. As my grandmother likes to say, *Zuòzhe chī*—sit and eat. I'm assuming you don't speak Chinese."

"I don't speak Chinese," Colton said at last, finding his voice. "But, 'sit and eat' I understand, and I'm starving. For whatever you're serving up... *Chef* Liu."

CHAPTER 3

*L*ater that night, sitting on the deck with a cup of tea and a light sweater around her shoulders, Liu watched the sun as it set behind the mountains. She'd unpacked nearly all afternoon, and exhaustion was hitting her hard; yet she wanted to savor the accomplishment of striking out on her own, and all that had transpired.

Liu propped her flip-flopped feet and tan legs on the deck railing and reflected on her first day as private chef for the West family—a coveted job she'd gotten by beating out a long list of applicants, including more conventional ranch cooks.

All in all, day one had gone well. The cook house was beyond beautiful. There was plenty of room for her family, who would visit often. The cupboards and pantry were stuffed with new dishes, glasses and mugs, serving platters, and the latest and greatest appliances—many still in boxes. She felt like a bride, surrounded by new wedding gifts.

"Complete with a good-looking man in my shower," Liu thought, laughing a bit at the memory of Colton's surprised expression.

And Colton West was *very* good looking.

He can take a shower here any old time... Liu started to think, but then checked herself. Colton was a member of the West family, and therefore her employer. As nice as he was, it wouldn't be right to assume too much familiarity. *She* would keep it professional. Even though he seemed as amiable as a golden retriever.

Liu wondered what it must be like to have such a carefree life. As chef Alex, from her favorite foodie show *Chopped* would say, "I'm having a different experience."

The only child of a Chinese family, Liu was expected to work hard and succeed. Even now, she felt guilty for not unpacking more, and could hear her mother's voice in her head telling her to "exceed expectations." At the same time she heard Kat West telling her to take her time settling in.

This summed up to a tee the cultures that sometimes warred in Liu's head.

When this happened, it was best to think of something neutral and happy. Which brought her back to Colton West. She'd only been in the house for ten minutes before he was sitting in her kitchen with his stomach rumbling. She could tell he was a man who was always hungry.

And oh, those eyes!

So hopeful and expectant as they watched her. There was something else there too, that she couldn't put her finger on.

She knew from Kat that Colton was single. He was near her age, maybe a few years older. Liu wondered if his family was as disappointed in his marital status as hers was. Surely, women were lined up for miles in West Gorge to take Colton West off the market.

Liu pictured Colton again, fresh out of the shower and sitting at her island. His short hair and partial beard glowed with sun-kissed tips. A thin plaid shirt clung tight to his muscular arms, probably because he'd dressed while still damp. The pearl-toned snaps were fastened most of the way up his chest, with a few undone near the top.

As he perched on a stool and leaned over, soft curls peeked out of Colton's open collar. At least, Liu assumed the curls were soft. For a crazy moment she longed to reach across and find out, but stopped herself. He probably wouldn't have minded; he seemed so agreeable.

But someone so agreeable could not be sensible, Liu concluded. That would not do.

"*Enough,*" she said out loud, admonishing herself for thinking like a silly school girl. It was pointless to be attracted to Colton West—someone her family would never condone.

Liu was used to navigating the Chen's very specific expectations, and calculated that she could get away with one big move that strayed from their approved path for her life—she could choose her own career, or choose her husband. But going for both could end in disaster.

So far, there wasn't any man in college or culinary school worth defying her family over. Now, they were growing anxious, and weren't exactly thrilled about her move to the ranch.

How are you going to meet somebody in the middle of nowhere?

By "somebody," they meant somebody Chinese. They had done their homework, and the Chinese community in West Gorge was small. So in order for the Chens to agree to this job, Liu found herself making… concessions. Ones she had been avoiding. These concessions made her nervous, but kept her family satisfied for the time being.

She'd worry about the implications later—there was enough on her mind. Like the West Ranch cowboys and their diet of gooey, heavy casseroles and burgers, and sticky sweet, creamy desserts. Kat asked her to change things up; to make the meals hearty but healthy. Liu had a lot of ideas, but the proof would be in the pudding.

Or rather, in the lo mein noodles.

Liu Chen watched the last of the sun drop behind the hills and the gorge. In the far-off distance, a train was passing through the valley, and with it a pack of howling coyotes. Her eyes fluttered heavily as she took a last deep breath of fresh mountain air. Tomorrow would be the beginning of an exciting new life.

She would work hard for the West family, and make them love her cooking.

One day, she would make her family proud of her.

And she would accept their choice for her husband—but defer

marriage for as long she could. Meanwhile, she'd hope and pray that whoever her husband was, *wherever* he was, he might look at her the way Colton West did.

With a slight shiver, Liu recalled the cowboy's sweet forbidden gaze, knowing she should try to erase it from her mind. What she didn't know, was how hard he was going to make it.

CHAPTER 4

"*A*shes to ashes, and dust to dust."

In his Sunday suit and bolo tie, the silver-haired pastor held his Bible in one hand, while looking solemnly at the West family as they stood outside in the late June sunshine. "We commit this body to the ground, earth to earth," he said. "We do this in sure and certain hope of the Resurrection to eternal life."

Turning to Ash Gibson West, the pastor gestured for the boy to proceed.

Ash swallowed hard and nodded at the pastor, then gently took a step forward. He silently and lovingly set a dozen white roses on top of the closed casket that held the remains of his precious departed grandmother.

Weeks before, her slight head cold had turned to pneumonia in her lungs, from which she couldn't recover.

The Alzheimer's disease that plagued her mind had already taken control of her body.

She could no longer remember her grandson's name, which hurt the boy. But by the same token, she couldn't remember the pain and suffering caused by Ash's mother—Granny's only child—who had abandoned young and old alike. She left them to care for each other while she crossed the border to Mexico to make a new life.

Running from God only knew what.

Granny had taken Ash in as a boy of eleven. In turn, Ash cared for her the only way he knew how, by trying to protect her from injuring herself, burning the house down, or neglecting to eat or pay her bills.

His well-meaning but youthful efforts caught up with him a few years ago, and he ended up in the hands of Gunnar West, who brought him home to West Ranch as a foster kid of 15. A year later, Ridge West, the patriarch of the family, adopted Ash as his fourth and youngest son.

Now, at 17, high school senior Ash West buried his blood kin, as Ridge's strong and loving hand rested upon the lad's drooping shoulder.

"She sure did love you, son," Ridge said through a lump in his throat.

"Yep," was all Ash could manage to say.

One by one, the others standing in the West family cemetery on the warm day set their own roses on the casket, as they said prayers for the dearly departed, and for the grieving Ash.

There was Gunnar and Kat, holding baby Willow.

Pike and Paislee West.

Ridge, of course, and Colton West.

Marta and Nels Scott were in attendance, along with their son, police officer Jason Scott, who had gotten close to Ash during his brief stay in the West Gorge jail. And a handful of nurses and doctors from the West Gorge Nursing Home who had lovingly cared for Granny.

Doctor Josh Quell was there, along with his fiancée.

A few of Ash's teachers and friends from the high school had come, too.

Ash was grateful for the turnout. There was a time, not so long ago, when he had been all alone in the world, but for Granny. He was comforted to see that was no longer the case. He would be sure to greet everyone individually.

"Good Lord, Ash," a quavering voice spoke as a dry and bony hand gripped his own before he could turn to follow the mourners to the luncheon, "I can't believe she's really gone!"

It was the familiar face he saw every time he checked up on Granny's house while she was in the nursing home—either peeking out from behind her lace curtains, or waving from the garden next door.

"Miss Emily," Ash said to Granny's neighbor, kissing her on the cheek, "thank you for coming. Granny would have wanted you here." Ash knew she'd gotten a ride to the funeral from Marta and Nels.

Nodding and bobbing her silvery head, Granny's ancient neighbor seemed unable to form her words. Her lips were moving as if trying to will her voice to catch up with her thoughts. Finally, she managed to form a sentence.

"I always thought she'd get better and come on home," Emily said, and then it was Ash's turn to nod.

"Me too, Miss Emily," he said. "Me too."

But Ash was just being polite. He had long ago accepted Granny would only get worse.

"Are you going to move back home now?" Emily asked, after nodding some more.

Ash turned and looked at her fully for the first time. Emily's skin was milky white, with blue veins showing through at her temples and neck. Her eyes looked clear, like glass marbles. And her hair was snowy and white, like cotton balls. She continued to nod and bob her head, as if she couldn't stop.

But her face was almost youthful with a sense of hope that someone would come home—if not Granny, then Ash.

"This ranch is my home now. But even if I wanted to, I... I don't think the house is mine to come home to," he told Granny's neighbor. "I'm sure the bank owns it now."

"Oh no," Emily stated as a fact. "It's yours. Your granny told me long ago."

A sad smile played on Ash's lips; Granny said a lot of things.

Maybe she told Emily that she was giving him the little bungalow, but more than once, she told Ash that dinner was ready, only to find an empty roasting pan in the oven. She also packed his school lunch with her car keys and a can of beans.

At some point, Granny's word had become unreliable. But when, he did not know.

"I guess I'll find out soon enough, Miss Emily," Ash said. "I don't think anybody knows how to get a hold of my mom."

"Oh, your grandma wouldn't give your mama the time of day, let alone her estate," Emily said. "It's worth a fortune."

Her estate.

Ash fought the urge to smile at the thought of Granny's little house, which was likely mortgaged to the hilt, as an *estate*. Estates, Ash knew, had grand entrances, multiple bathrooms, and butler's pantries —like the West Ranch house. Not small eat-in kitchens with green and gold appliances, and pink Formica counter tops in the powder rooms.

But he didn't want Emily to think he was making fun of her, so he nodded solemnly.

"I'll let you know what I find out, Miss Emily," Ash said. "For now, let's walk on over together to have some lunch."

Ash held out his arm for the elderly neighbor and friend of Granny, and the two walked slowly towards the outdoor covered pavilion used for West family events and community gatherings. The tables were set with red and white checked linens, with vases of wild-flowers in the center. At the back, a long serving table was filled with food from Red's Rib Shack, and cakes from the bakery in town.

One of the last to go through the line was Colton, who waited until everyone had filled their plates so he could linger. Liu, he was pleased to see, made a point of waiting on him.

"Hungry?" She asked.

"Always," he said.

The West's new chef, Liu Chen, wore a spotless apron and directed a half dozen others in aprons as they served guests and refreshed cups of coffee and glasses of lemonade.

"*Qīnglǐ*," Liu quietly admonished her staff in both Chinese and English, "clean up as you go!"

CHAPTER 5

*C*olton sat a few tables away from the food buffet, but he still flinched every time Liu delicately but firmly gave her orders. Without realizing it, he found himself using a paper napkin to wipe a lemonade ring from the tablecloth.

For such a tiny thing, Liu had a big presence, Colton thought. He felt compelled to do whatever she said, without complaint.

Only a few days into her new job, Liu had rallied to pull together the funeral luncheon. Kat mentioned to the family that Liu had insisted on cooking from scratch. Kat both commended, and dissuaded her.

"Oh goodness Liu," Kat had told the chef. "Even Justice, with his freezer full of meals, would need more than a few days' notice to feed a small army. Everyone will be thrilled with Red's ribs, and cakes from the bakery."

Liu, she could tell, felt she had failed at her first big task as the West family chef. But everyone knew that the ranch cook had barely unpacked her own suitcase, let alone the big kitchen, when news had come of Granny's death.

"Besides, Red is practically family—he's one of my husband's oldest friends," Kat assured Liu. "It blesses their business to cater our events. Especially those with no notice, like funerals."

Randi West's funeral, Kat knew, had been catered by Red's Rib Shack in the banquet room of the large church in town—spilling out to tables and chairs in the parking lot. A few hundred locals had been in attendance, and Gunnar didn't think it was a coincidence that Red could afford to take his wife Jackie to Yellowstone, to the pricey Old Faithful Inn, soon after.

No one begrudged Red and Jackie the windfall.

"A heartbreaking funeral like that makes a fellow want to hold tight to his sweetie every chance he can," Ridge had said at the time.

Kat was glad to see a respectable turnout for Granny, for Ash's sake. She and Ash joined the West family around the same time, and their lives had both changed for the better. Kat imagined how scared and lonely Ash would have been, burying his grandmother as an abandoned teenager, living in foster care.

But now as Ash West, he had a father who was staying close, providing comfort and strength. He had new brothers who were doing the same. He had sisters to dote and love on him, and help him through the worst of his grief—and a baby niece to make him smile. He had a home to take solace in and family to surround him.

Looking around at stories being told, and at the laughter and tears shared around the tables, Kat wondered what her own funeral would have been like, had she died of the ResVi virus that swept through Wyoming just a short few years ago—before she married Gunnar.

Poor Josh Quell, who she barely knew at the time, would have shipped her remains back to Illinois, where her lone mother would bury her and singly mourn her loss. Her father, Jack Tate, abandoned them when Kat was just an adolescent.

The thought was so sad, she found a few new tears rolling down her cheeks. Quickly, Gunnar was by her side with his arm around her shoulder.

"Are you thinking about Ash and Granny?" he asked.

Kat shook her head.

"I should be, but I'm thinking about *me*..." she cried in response, "dying. Without ever having married you, Gunnar. Wouldn't that just be so sad?"

"It would be sad," Gunnar nodded, choosing his words carefully. Being new to married life, he marveled at how women could make themselves cry at the drop of a hat, over things that never actually happened. It was just one of the pitfalls he was learning to navigate as a husband.

"*Hey*, let's get you some cake!" He said, and thankfully, Kat agreed.

A short while later, after most everyone said their goodbyes, the immediate West family made their way to the little family cemetery for a private burial service. As Ash tossed a handful of dirt on the box, he wondered if his mother would object to Granny being here on West land, instead of at the public cemetery, but then decided he just didn't care.

You never came to see her when she was alive, Ash yelled at her in his mind, pushing his mother's objections down into the dirt with the heel of his boot.

Giving his head a slight shake, he knew he had to bring this up in his next session at the hospital. His therapist had been helping him work through his past and his pain, to avoid having them manifest into unsavory actions—like stealing money.

After the burial, and saying goodbye to the pastor who had presided over the day, the West family strolled together to the big house. Ash was flanked by Ridge and Colton. Little Willow slept on Gunnar's shoulder. Kat walked beside them, her arm through the crook in her husband's own. Newlyweds Pike and Paislee held hands and brought up the rear.

Upon entering the ranch kitchen, exhausted from the day, they were greeted by a platter of sesame chicken skewers atop a mound of fresh Asian slaw, next to a separate plate of warm dumplings and a sweet and sour sauce.

On a glass pedestal stood a white cake from the bakery, with orange zest icing. Next to it, a tall carafe held iced honeyed tea.

A note from Liu leaned against a vase of flowers, welcoming the family home.

"Yum!" Paislee exclaimed, and Kat agreed. "How thoughtful," she said.

The men nodded begrudgingly. They were hungry, but were also lamenting no doubt, the absence of the cheesier, meatier, heartier casseroles—the "gut bomb" comfort dishes they'd gotten used to in the past thirty years.

Even more so in the past five years, since the passing away of menu gatekeeper Randi West.

But not one of the men dared question Kat's hiring decision, lest she point her little finger and send them all packing to Cindy's Diner for yet another cheeseburger. They were the best burgers in town, but the men had eaten far too many in the past weeks.

"*Yum,* indeed," Ridge chimed in, hoping he sounded sincere.

SITTING around the large ranch table, having changed from their suits and dresses into tee shirts and jeans, the West family was about to retire to their own rooms when the phone jarred them. Ridge answered on the third ring.

"Ridge West," he said. And then, "yep, yep, yep. I see."

Ridge looked over at Ash.

"Yes, I reckon Ash and I can be there tomorrow at noon," he said.

Ash's eyebrows raised.

When Ridge hung up, he came to sit back down. Everyone's curiosity was peaked, and nobody moved.

"Ash," he said, "you and I have an appointment tomorrow. With your grandmother's attorney."

Ash frowned.

"Granny... had an *attorney?*"

CHAPTER 6

*C*olton slowly approached the ranch cook house a few mornings later, driving his Range Rover. A sensation in his gut surprised him—it felt like butterflies. He'd never been nervous before coming up to this building. Justice came on board when Colton was still in his mother's arms. One of his earliest memories was toddling to the cook house for a snack. Another was stretching out on the shaded front deck as a little boy to take his naps.

Randi West always knew where to look for Colton.

Now, Colton got out of his car and took a minute to straighten his shirt. He removed his cowboy hat before climbing the stairs to the front door—a door he'd never knocked on before.

"Come in," Liu's voice called out, before Colton had even rapped once. As he opened the door, he could see Liu standing behind the stainless-steel work table. She barely looked up. When she did, a small smile played on her lips.

"Sit," she commanded.

Colton removed his boots and left them on the rug, then gingerly perched on one of the stools.

"Thank you for taking off your boots," Liu said. "It's very rude to wear shoes in Asian households. But in America, people walk in and out without a thought, tracking who-knows-what on their soles."

"You're welcome," Colton said.

"What brings you here, cowboy—hungry?" Liu said, placing a plate of fresh spring rolls in front of Colton. "Here, dip those in this hot and sour sauce I just made."

"I'm always hungry," he said, although he had just eaten breakfast. Colton did as he was told, then quickly drew in a sharp breath to cool off his mouth.

"*Whoo!* That's spicy! As my dad would say, that'll grow hair on your chest!" he exclaimed between gulps of air.

Liu smiled as she continued to chop vegetables.

"As I recall," she said, "you don't need any more hair on your chest."

"Ah hah," Colton laughed, "then your glasses weren't as fogged up as I'd hoped when you caught me in the shower the other day."

Liu smiled along with him. "I confess to having pretty good eyesight. My glasses are mostly a fashion accessory."

Colton noticed she wasn't wearing glasses just then, and her eyes sparkled with good humor as they bantered.

"Yes, I noticed your chest, Colton. Asian men have literally *no* chest hair," she went on. "They are as smooth and silky as the beautiful jade carvings in my grandmother's room."

Colton winced. "That's new information," he said, "that I really didn't need to know."

"Plus, you wore only a very small towel," she said with a laugh in her voice.

"I wore the towel you handed me—and I'll bet you have larger ones," he said.

"I might," she said with a smile. "But naked beggars caught in the shower can't be choosy. Now, what brings you here this morning?"

Colton tilted his head as he watched her masterfully chop, moving her hands deftly as she put the vegetables in a variety of containers. He had watched old Justice do his food prep a million times, wildly chopping at carrots and celery like he was trying to corral and kill a bunch of snakes that were trying to slither off the table.

Liu Chen—*Chef* Liu—was vastly more refined and in control. Her movements were purposeful, and economical. And sexy, truth be told.

"Kat sent me over to return your cake plate," he said, "and to thank you for your hard work at the funeral. And for the family meal you left us."

Liu looked up with a note of skepticism in her eyes. To her ears, he seemed to be throwing reasons at a wall, hoping one would stick.

"Cake plate, huh," she said.

They both knew Colton was fibbing about that. Kat said she'd place any serving pieces of Liu's in the butler's pantry for her to retrieve at her convenience. But she didn't call him out. He was trying hard, and he was awfully cute doing so.

"And…" he went on, "to see if you'd like to go for a drive with me. I can show you more of West Ranch if you'd like, or we could go into town. I thought maybe you'd like to see West Gorge Woods, the housing development I'm heading up."

She stopped chopping and regarded Colton closely. He had just taken another bite of a spring roll, and stopped mid chew as she sized him up. In that moment, he felt like a school kid on picture day, when Randi would squint at him with her "eagle-eyes," assessing him for flaws, and checking his shirt for stains and smudges.

He held still and sat a little straighter, trying not to breath as she made her determination.

"Very well," Liu said at last. "I'll let you drive me to Red's Rib Shack. I need to return some chafing dishes from the funeral, and I've never been there."

"We could have lunch," Colton said hopefully, with half a spring roll still in his hand.

"It's ten in the morning," she pointed out, gesturing to the clock on the wall with her knife. "You're eating spring rolls." Her knife turned to point at the plate in front of him.

"We'll take the long way, and kill some time," he said. "But I can always eat."

Liu rolled her eyes just a little, but retained the smile, which

Colton found promising. She turned her knife tip towards a few boxes for Red, and asked Colton to load them in his car. She would put away the vegetables and change her clothes.

CHAPTER 7

"She what?"

"You heard right." Sitting in his paneled office in downtown West Gorge, attorney Max Fielder repeated himself to a flabbergasted Ash, who sat next to Ridge on the other side of his pine desk.

"Your grandmother put her house in your name, as well as your grandfather's pension, their stocks, and her savings account," he said. "It all adds up to quite a small fortune—especially for a young man of your age."

As Ash and Ridge examined the spreadsheet that contained the numbers, Max continued.

"Of course, the title of the house remains in a trust until you become 18 years of age, but that's just around the corner. The courts would want you to be of-age to sell the property."

"Sell it…" Ash snapped to attention at that comment.

"I work with a local realtor, Casey Parks," Max said. "She could make quick work of listing your grandmother's house, and getting you top dollar—when you're ready, that is. Property values in West Gorge have skyrocketed in the past few years."

"The house is the only thing I have left of my blood kin," Ash said.

Ridge reached over and patted Ash on his leg to reassure him.

"No worries," Max said. "The escrow will cover property taxes and utilities until you are ready to make a decision."

Ash looked at Ridge, who was letting the boy absorb the enormity of his Granny's legacy.

"My condolences on losing your grandmother, Ash. But that aside, I have to say that owning property in West Gorge is enviable," Max ventured. "The vacation rental business is booming."

"Is that so?" Ridge spoke at last, his curiosity peaked.

"Jackson Hole has gotten very pricey for tourists, but people are still coming to Wyoming in droves—so they're branching out to West Gorge, Pinedale, and Cody. Folks are vacationing in the Bighorns and the Wind River range—not just the Tetons anymore. Casey Parks said she gets calls every day from people wanting to rent by the week, or even the month. I wish I'd hopped on the rental market when these little houses were still within reach," Max answered.

He looked directly at Ash as he finished his thought.

"If you don't want to sell, you could make a tidy sum by renting out your grandmother's house, Ash," he said, "providing you update it just a bit. But then again, you've got your last year of high school to think about, and then college. You may not want the hassle."

Ash nodded, distractedly. So did Ridge. A row of houses just a block off of Main Street had caught Ridge's eye recently—each painted an inviting color, and each with a discreet sign that read: *Rent a Parks Place!*

They must be owned by this Casey Parks, who was apparently buying up the town—the town Ridge's own great grandfather built. It got his hackles up, knowing that some upstart was getting her claws in the homes meant for the hard-working citizens of West Gorge. Now, these same citizens would be hard pressed to afford their own home. While the Casey Parks of the world pushed them out.

"In the meantime," Max said, sliding a set of house keys across the desk, "here are the keys. Just let me know what you want to do, and where you want me to put all your money."

The men stood and shook hands and agreed on next steps. Ash

tucked the keys in his pocket before walking out. In the late June sunshine, Ash looked at Ridge and jingled the keys.

"Will you come with me... Dad?"

Ridge put his arm on Ash's shoulder and squeezed hard, while swallowing a lump in his throat. The older West truly loved the boy, and could barely remember what life was like without him. And with Gunnar, Pike and Colton grown and on their own, all heading in their own directions, Ridge was pleased to be able to help the young Ash navigate these difficult years—and be needed again.

"Let's go," Ridge said, walking to the Jeep.

A few minutes later, Ridge and Ash were walking towards Granny's little bungalow, when Miss Emily intercepted them. She came out from behind a hedge, tottering at a fast clip.

"Man, she's surprisingly fast," Ash whispered to Ridge. He had hoped to avoid another lengthy conversation—just this once.

"See Ash, I told you so, didn't I?" Emily pointed her walking cane right at him. Ash stepped back to avoid being poked in the eye.

"You were right, Miss Emily," Ash said. "Now if you'll excuse us..."

"That real estate woman was sniffing around here today," Emily kept talking. "She came knocking at my door, wanting me to sell my house. *Sell* my *house*, I say! Do I look like I'm going *anywhere*, Ash?"

Truthfully, Ash thought Emily did look like someone who shouldn't be living alone, but he kept this to himself.

"I sent her over to the house on the other side of you," Emily told the men. "It's been empty for nearly a year. The Madison's lived there last, but they high-tailed it up to Missoula to take a job in oil."

Ridge looked over at the empty house, and decided to see what he could find out. He had a little money—well, okay, he had a lot of money—and maybe he might want to get into the rental market himself.

If for no other reason than to beat this Casey Parks to the punch!

He thought about Pickford and Addie West, back in the late 1800s. They had to scramble to not only hang onto their land, but expand it every chance they had. Once they filed a homestead claim on adjacent property, they were required to build dwellings, and cultivate the land, documenting their improvements as they went.

They had to battle the land speculators, who often took advantage of pioneers and homesteaders by reselling the land at fraudulent, exorbitant prices. Good people broke their backs supporting themselves, until the time when the land supported them.

They had to build houses and barns where there was little if any timber. Living first in dugouts—a scooped cave in the side of a hill—then in huts made from dried dung. Both of these were easily washed away in a good rain, and were always filthy. Still, they sheltered entire households until a time when a more permanent dwelling could be built.

They dug primitive wells, and tried to stay warm during long cold winters, with very little available fuel. Homesteading both ignited and killed the dreams of many who were miserable, cold, isolated, and hungry.

People often died.

Their animals didn't always fare much better.

Ridge had been raised on stories of these high-spirited pioneers, and in his own heyday, had secured the boundaries of West Ranch and expanded his family's holdings. He'd also given land to the community. The land near the gorge, for example—he put that in a public trust for hiking and camping. And he donated land for hospitals, and the new cancer center.

And soon, the West Gorge Arts and Culture Center.

But maybe it was time to remind the Casey Parks of the world just whose town this was, before everyone thought of him as going "soft."

A smile spread slowly on his face, then he turned to follow Ash into his Granny's bungalow. Ash's bungalow, now.

CHAPTER 8

"*I* like sharing ribs with you," Colton said, wiping his fingers on a napkin. To his surprise and delight, Liu only ate two of the sauce-slathered ribs, leaving the rest for him. She preferred the slaw and beans, she said.

"I'm more of a savory sides girl," Liu quipped.

They were sitting at a wooden picnic table on Red's outdoor patio by the river.

Liu smiled at Colton, and companionably ate another bite of the lunch that Red and Jackie insisted they have when they came to deliver the serving pans.

"I eat meat, but not in the quantities you Americans do," she said. "I think of meat as more of a side dish. I prefer vegetables and grains."

Colton nodded and regarded her.

"Wait a minute," he said, "you said 'you Americans' but you were born in Wyoming, right?"

To him, she looked very American in her cropped jeans, vintage Fleetwood Mac tee shirt, and brightly woven river sandals with criss-crossed straps. And like every good Wyoming girl, her turquoise and sterling earrings hung down and jangled like bells in the slight breeze.

And unless she was using Chinese words while talking to her staff, she sounded as American as any girl he'd ever known.

"Yes," Liu said, "I am fourth-generation Chinese-American, with very little emphasis on the *American,* according to my family."

"And why is that?" Colton truly wanted to know.

"That's easy," Liu said, "American ways are more... self-centered than Chinese ways. Americans are rugged individuals, I suppose. A trait that's not cool in a Chinese family."

Colton nodded.

"I'm already rebelling by not being married by my 'sell by' age of 23," Liu said with a wry smile, "I passed that a few years ago. Soon, I will be a *leftover woman,* one who brings dishonor by not bringing grandchildren into the family."

Liu said this in a lighthearted tone, but Colton wondered how much the revelation pained her to confess.

"Well if you ask me, there's nothing *leftover* about you, Liu," Colton said, shaking his head. "You are fresh and young, and very beautiful. I'd say your life is just getting started."

Liu flinched at the cowboy's words, and she dropped her gaze. She was not used to compliments, he was certain.

"Thank you, Colton," she said, and then added playfully, "if only you were Chinese, I could bring *you* home."

"You don't think your family would fall in love with me?" he asked, playing along.

Liu shook her head. "Sorry, no. I think you're used to people loving you, Colton, but you're not Chinese. And you're the youngest son. Bad luck combination."

"Ah, but you're wrong there. I am no longer the youngest son," Colton replied in good humor, "not since my Dad adopted Ash. My prospects are looking up."

Liu smiled at him. "Still not Chinese, though. If I brought you home, I could no longer be a chef—I'd have to go to law school."

"Well you lost me there, but that's a lot of pressure they place on you," Colton continued, more seriously.

To Liu, he seemed enraptured by the cultural differences between them.

"No biggee," Liu shrugged. "I embody all my parents' and grand-parents' hopes and dreams. But I've never known anything different."

Colton watched her carefully. He could sense a growing tension, and longed to diffuse it.

"Hey, hungry still?" Colton pointing to the food on a tray. "What else would you like?"

Liu looked at his pointing hand and then caught his eyes. She gently reached over and placed her hands on both of his.

"Let me show you," she said. With Colton's hands in both her own, she turned them over, palm sides up. Tenderly, she smoothed open his fingers as if buttering two slices of bread.

Her hands were small and soft, but to Colton her touch felt electric. He sensed the nerves throughout his entire body reacting to her feather-soft fingers.

"We never point with one finger. We gesture with open hands and palms up," Liu said.

As he kept his palms up like he was holding an open book, Liu moved her own hands gracefully through the air. Her gestures were so beautiful, Colton was spellbound.

"Let me try again," Colton said. He then gestured to the food with both of his open hands, asking Liu if she would like any more to eat.

"A biscuit, please," she said, smiling broadly at the cowboy.

Using a napkin, Colton held a roll out with both open hands for Liu, and she took it.

"Xiè xie," Liu said and nodded. "Thank you. And thank you for driving me to Red's today."

"I'm glad I came with you," Colton teased, "because I'm pretty sure Red made you a job offer while he thought I wasn't looking. You've hardly unpacked, and they want to steal you from the ranch."

Liu laughed.

"He did say I could come run their operation anytime I wanted," she said. "But don't worry, I was born in the year of the dog, and I am very loyal. Being a private chef for the West family is a wonderful opportunity and I'm grateful to Kat. I take my job very seriously."

"Then I'd better get you back to the cook house, Chef Liu," Colton said with a slight bow. "But first, let me say *shee shee*; thank you for coming out with me today."

"Colton, you're a nut," Liu said.

Silently, Colton grimaced.

That wasn't the first time he'd heard that. But hearing Liu talk about her family, and their serious ambitions for her, Colton caught his first glimmer of wanting to be something much more than a *nut* in her eyes.

CHAPTER 9

*A*fter dropping Liu off, Colton made his way back into town, towards West Gorge Woods. He needed to check on the homes being built, and the restaurants. A county inspector was meeting him later to approve the progress his company, West Development, had been making.

Now that Pike and Paislee's home was complete—in record time, Colton was proud to say—the crew could focus their efforts on the other buildings. It was nearly July, and they would only have another two or three months before the first snowfall.

Expectations were very high; families were waiting to move into the new neighborhood, and closer to the newest schools.

Colton's days started before sunrise, and didn't end until after dark.

"We can sleep this winter," he told the men on the crew.

Wyoming summers were usually dry and sunny, once the last of the snow melted in the sweeping basin at the foot of the hills. When winter came around again, the weather was unrelenting. All work would move inside the buildings, providing the men could reach them through the blowing and drifting snow.

"But today," Colton said out the open window of his Range Rover, "the sun is shining."

As he drove, he thought of his outing with Liu, and some of her comments.

"I'm sure you're used to people loving you," she had said.

He didn't think she was being malicious or mean—and honestly, she was right. Colton had a reputation for being jocular and fun-loving. When he walked into a room, he was received with smiles and laughter. Men clapped him on the back. Women grabbed his arm, and smiled up at his tanned face and sun-bleached hair, as if they'd been waiting for him their whole lives.

When he picked girls up in West Gorge for dates, their parents greeted him like a hero.

"Why, Colton West! Aren't you a sight for sore eyes," they would gush.

"You kids have fun," they'd insist, never questioning where they were going, or for how long.

He *was* loved wherever he went. And when Randi was alive, she was his biggest fan.

Colton would watch as Randi and Gunnar had early morning chats on the big deck of the ranch, and witnessed the many secret conversations between Randi and Pike over the years. But when his mother saw him enter a room, she lit up like a Christmas tree.

"You have been a joy to me, Colton," Randi would say. "Starting on the day you were born, and every day since."

She told him that the third child is pure delight, and that's what he aimed to be for her. He didn't have to try very hard, he discovered. Randi just loved and adored Colton, he knew, unconditionally. She was always ready to laugh at his jokes and smile at his antics. Even when she became ill—especially then.

They had serious talks, too.

"Don't accept anything in life that threatens to break your spirit, Colton," she told him in her last months. "Your spirit is not superficial as some might suggest, it's your great gift."

Colton wished his mother was alive so he could talk to her about Liu. Thinking about her tiny hands, and the way she taught him the Chinese custom for giving and receiving—the sparks he felt at her gentle touch—he didn't want to roll over and accept that her heart was off limits.

People did love him, and there was no reason the serious Chen family couldn't love him, too. If Liu would agree to go on a few dates, he would be determined to win their favor.

How hard could that be?

"YES MAMA," Liu said as she chopped vegetables back at the cook house. Liu's phone sat on the work station as the two talked through a speaker. She had been telling her mother about the well-appointed cook house, the funeral luncheon, and her trip to West Gorge with Colton.

Liu learned at an early age that there was no privacy afforded a child in a Chinese household. All four adults were in her business day and night, probing into all of her activities, her grades in school—and even her friends and *their* grades in school. Liu could not spend time with friends who did not take school seriously. They might lead her astray.

The Chens insisted on a full account of her hopes, dreams, and snacks from sunup to sundown. Being out on her own was no different.

Only now, with no one looking over her shoulder, she dared to keep a few details to herself—like how handsome Colton West was, and how she found herself flirting with him just a little. Something she'd never done before, but couldn't seem to help when he was near.

Though very little escaped the Chen women.

"Your grandmother wants you to watch out for cowboys, Liu," her mother cautioned her. "She asks that you remember what they did in 1885."

"Yes Mama," Liu said again, shaking her head a little. There was no use reminding her mother or grandmother that it wasn't the cowboys who caused the Rock Springs massacre of Chinese coal miners. It was fellow coal miners working for the Union Pacific Railroad who had attacked them.

Times had become hard, and jobs in the West were scarce. These workers tried to drive the immigrant miners out of Wyoming after becoming convinced they were being favored—when the opposite was true. They made less money in the mines, and paid more for housing.

The treatment of Chinese long ago was truly terrible, Liu couldn't deny. It made her grandparents fearful, and her parents wary, so of course it affected her too. But keeping suspicion alive was tiring. She longed for a slightly more modern life of hope, and optimism. While being mindful that her ancestors had paid a steep price so she could hope.

CHAPTER 10

"*N*ai Nai," was one of the first names Liu learned to say as a very small girl.

Grandmother.

It was Chun, her father's mother, who taught Liu to cook when she was young. While her mother and father worked long days—her father Zhang as a software engineer, and her mother Ling as an accountant—Chun raised Liu and cared for the home.

Chun's great love, besides Liu, was cooking. At one time she ran a restaurant in Rock Springs, and prepared authentic Chinese dishes. People would come for miles to eat her food, and she passed this love to little Liu.

"*Oi Liu*," her grandmother would cluck at her—encouraging her to cut tiny onion stems with a small plastic knife for their breakfast of scallion pancakes. Different from the sweet maple syrup pancakes that her friends were used to eating, the Chens ate these savory, crispy little pancakes with a soy dipping sauce.

If there were any left, Liu ate them for an after-school snack.

Liu remembered feeling so important, being trusted with a dull butter knife and tiny wood cutting board. Her mother made her an apron, and a billowy chef's hat—and she was hooked.

Next, Chun taught Liu to make a fried rice for dinner, using the leftovers they had on hand. She would put chunks of cooked chicken on Liu's cutting board, which she would methodically dice for the meal. Then they would add more scallions, and peas. And Chun would have Liu crack eggs into a bowl and whisk them until they were creamy.

"Xiè xie," Chun would nod and smile at Liu while thanking her—which was the best feeling in the world for the little girl.

Chun herself would fry the meal, as the hot oil and flames were dangerous. But Liu was patient, waiting until her grandmother allowed her to take more responsibility.

As they cooked together, Chun shared stories with Liu about the men who came to work for the railroad, who were lonely because they made too little money to send for their families.

While her American friends and classmates were learning nursery rhymes about cows jumping over the moon, and how to skip rope while singing *Miss Mary Mack*, Liu heard frightening tales about the scarcity of jobs in Wyoming for Chinese workers.

Chun told her that when they were treated badly by angry people long ago, the Chinese community was able to survive and rebuild what was taken from them only by sticking together. Which is why they needed to continue sticking together.

Over stir frying and chopping and seasoning, Liu made a promise that she would show respect by marrying a Chinese man when she grew up.

Yes Nai Nai.

Of course, Nai Nai.

It was a promise she hadn't questioned, until now.

The cowboys Liu knew were as nice as could be—especially the West family. According to Colton, his own ancestors came to Wyoming to escape the Pennsylvania mines. They were a kind, hard-working family, and very down to earth.

Much like the Chens.

Also like the Wests, the Chens live with multiple generations under one roof.

Liu's father works remotely from an office in their house, and his parents, Chun and Tao, share the family home. Grandmother Chun prepares the meals, while elder Tao drinks tea in the garden and cultivates the trees and plants. On weekends, they all play Mahjong and discuss Liu's future while anticipating her next visit. Each as eager as the next for her to move back home, along with a husband and babies.

Culinary school threw her family a curve ball, Liu knew. She had to first earn her degree in business before even broaching the topic. And then it took a lot of gentle persuading.

In the Chinese community, being a chef was still considered a default career. Cooking was the one thing their ancestors did when no other options were available. When education wasn't a possibility. To have Liu want to become a chef when there was ample money set aside for law school or medical school, made the Chens very nervous.

Eventually, they became supportive—*ish*. Probably, Liu figured, because they thought it might someday make her a better wife. Still Zhang and Ling, and Chun and Tao took comfort knowing that while Liu was unconventional, she was never rebellious or disrespectful. She honored the dead, and the family hierarchy.

And she had agreed to fly to China to meet a man of her auntie's choosing.

This brought the Chens much happiness.

CHAPTER 11

"*W*ait, whoa, *wait*," Pike implored. "Not so fast!"

"But it's our first day and night in our new home," Paislee pleaded excitedly as Pike held her back. "Why can't I go running inside?"

They had just unlocked their front door and swung it wide open. A scent hit them both—the sweet aromas of new paint, fresh wood floors, and their future together. Standing on the porch, Pike and Paislee smiled at each other, and leaned in to share a kiss.

Paislee was beautiful in a short lilac linen prairie dress, and white strappy sandals. Since their wedding, and their winter honeymoon in the remote barn, she had adopted a new and more confident style. Not so conservative. A little more colorful and Boho Chic. Pike adored the way she dressed, and wondered at how she pulled together her signature look with a combination of online orders, flea market baubles, and *finds* from the town outfitters.

"Because... this!" He said.

At that, Pike swept Paislee up in his arms and carried her across the threshold of their new modern farmhouse. As she laughed with delight, Pike carried her into the main rooms, each boasting a few pieces of new furniture, and twirled her around. Just has he twirled her on the day he proposed back in Denver.

"Welcome home, Mrs. West," Pike declared.

Before long, the two were laughing hard, and dizzy at the twirling. They fell into each other's arms. Quickly, the laughter turned to tears of joy. Pike set Paislee down, then kissed his wife's face and hair and hands until their kisses became something much more.

As they embraced, the warm scent of each other's lips and faces began to co-mingle with the scent of the oiled cherry hardwoods, and the permanence of the hammered Rocky Mountain hardware in every room of their own home—creating an aromatic christening that was nothing less than intoxicating. It was a dedication to their home and to each other that they could never explain; and a moment they would never forget.

With her body pressed against his own, and her tanned arms wrapped around his neck, the world fell away for Pike. He whispered as much in her ear.

"But the ice cream..." Paislee protested without conviction, as Pike ran his hands along her bare arms.

Their car was packed with groceries, and the front porch was covered with boxes and bags filled with wedding gifts, dishes, and suitcases.

"Let it melt," Pike said. His hand, which had been embracing her through the soft linen, traveled up her back to her neck, where he caressed her while holding loosely onto her curls.

The following morning, dressed in a white eyelet bathrobe, Paislee opened their front door. Stepping outside to take deep breaths of the fresh air, she stretched her arms as high and as wide as they would go, then began carrying in the forgotten packages.

"What *will* the neighbors think?" She asked Pike with a smile, as he walked onto the porch to help Paislee begin the job of moving in. He was barefoot, wearing faded jeans and an equally faded blue tee shirt that fit snugly against his chest.

Paislee thought that if a man were to have the equivalent of a lace nightie, this would be the outfit. *And he has no idea how good he looks,* she thought to herself, which made him even more attractive.

They both stopped and surveyed West Gorge Woods, and their silent corner of the undeveloped property. New houses were going up, true, but they were on the other side of the development, far from the newlywed's beautiful new home.

"By the time we have neighbors anywhere near us," Pike predicted, "you and I will have *ten* children running around our yard, and you'll be a frazzled house frau, screaming at everybody while waving a rolling pin, and not caring in the least what anyone thinks about us."

Paislee laughed at the image.

"Ten children," she said. "That's ambitious."

Pike gave his sweet bride a squeeze, then leaned over to whisper a suggestion into her ear.

"Stop, you," she said, "we need to start unpacking. But first..."

"Yes?" Pike asked, hopefully.

"Coffee!"

"Perfect. That's exactly what I hoped you'd say." Pike said.

As Paislee walked to the kitchen with bags filled with table linens for the butler's pantry, she murmured, "ten children, eh?"

Pike raised his eyebrows with an unspoken innuendo, and they both laughed.

Paislee hadn't thought of becoming pregnant, or not becoming pregnant, since she and Pike married. They both wanted children in due time, but were enjoying this honeymoon phase immensely. Neither were anxious to see it end.

Not to mention, Paislee had her hands full procuring the exhibits that would grace the walls of the West Gorge Arts and Culture Center —something that demanded her full attention. When Pike didn't demand it, that is.

So Paislee was okay deferring babies for a year or so. Still, she couldn't help wondering if something was amiss.

Kat was pregnant within months of marrying Pike's older brother Gunnar. And nobody in the family would wish little Willow away. She was the pride of her parents, and her aunts and uncles loved her to pieces. So did Grampa Ridge.

On paper, the pregnancy cut Kat and Gunnar's honeymoon short, but Kat and Gunnar didn't seem to get that memo. The two carried on like a couple of teenagers, Paislee noted. Just like she and Pike had been carrying on these past nine months.

"It will happen when it's meant to," Pepper Andrews, Paislee's mother, said. But that didn't stop Pepper from calling every month like clockwork, and asking her eldest daughter: "What's *New?*" Suggestively stretching out the word *new*, every time.

"Subtle much?" Paislee wanted to jab at her mother. But it was hard for Pepper to have Paislee living so far from Denver, she knew. So the daughter let her mother grill her at regular intervals, without holding back any news back.

But so far, there wasn't even a hint of an impending baby.

"Nothing is new, Mum," she had said to her very recently. "Oh... except I cooked a new dish last night. Chicken Tika Masala."

"Hmm," Pepper said in her disappointment. "Sounds gassy."

CHAPTER 12

"Your numbers add up," Ridge West said.

He and Ash were sitting at the table looking at a spread sheet Ash created in his AP summer business class. He was estimating how much money he would have to invest in the bungalow to make it a desirable rental, and how much he could expect to make back in the current market.

"The updates are mostly cosmetic," Ash told Ridge. "Granny took care of structural updates as needed, much to my surprise."

Ash thought his grandmother didn't have two pennies to rub together. But he understood now that she was hiding away her assets so that her ne'er-do-well daughter wouldn't come sniffing around for more handouts.

And while Ash was sorry Granny died, it would have destroyed him to see his mother swoop back in town and take control of Granny's assets, only to run the hard-earned life savings into the ground with her misdeeds and mismanagement.

"It makes me sad that Granny lived so meagerly," Ash told Ridge, who nodded at the boy.

"She lived like a queen, Ash," Ridge said, "because she had you in her life."

Ash dropped his head.

"Trust me," Ridge said as he placed his warm hand on Ash's shoulder, "taking care of the people we love is far more important than having money in the bank. But she made sacrifices in order to give you these gifts. And you'll honor her by remembering all she did, and why."

"So my parents wouldn't get their greedy hands on her money," Ash said, bitterly.

Ridge tightened his lips but didn't respond. His son was working through his anger, he knew. It would take time, and he would stay by his side. Be there when the lad needed him.

"Now then," Ridge said, changing the energy back to positive, "what's the plan?"

Ash sniffed, then smiled a slow mischievous grin.

"We're gonna turn the bungalow into the most sought-after little rental house in town," he said, "and give that realtor a run for her money."

"That's my boy," Ridge said with a hoot and a clap.

Later, thinking about the charming little row of *Parks Place Rentals* in town, Ridge called the town's office of deeds and land holdings. He asked to speak with Patricia, an old friend of his, about a plot he was starting to hatch.

"Now Ridge," she said, "you know I can't give you information that's not public yet. The Madison property has been empty, it's true. Bank-owned, I know that much."

"Patricia..." Ridge pleaded.

"Nope. No sir," she said with a jolly laugh. "You'd have me lose my job over a tiny house, when you own half the town already."

"Can you throw me a bone?" he asked her.

"Tell you what," Patricia said. "Only because it'll be public record tomorrow, I can tell you to register with a certain real estate auction company. The house is going to the highest bidder in about a week's time."

"You're the best," Ridge said.

"This conversation never happened," Patricia answered, and hung up.

If I can get my hands on the Madison house, Ridge started to think, then I can work side by side with Ash, and develop our own row of rental houses.

CHAPTER 13

"Colton, I need help."

The text on his phone came from Liu's private phone number. She had been at the ranch for three weeks now. Their paths crossed every now and then, but Colton had long days and early starts, as did Liu. Often when he came home, he'd find a special plate of dinner waiting for him in the refrigerator of the big house, with a sticky note on top of the foil lid.

"Are you okay?" he asked Liu in return. He was at the West Gorge Woods development, which was a long drive from the ranch. "Are you injured?"

Colton was truly alarmed to think Liu might be hurt, and he was ready to call the town's emergency hotline, then make a dash back to the ranch. She wielded that pointy knife far too freely in his estimation.

There was a pause, and he could see from the bouncing dots that she was typing her answer. She was either typing an awful lot, or thinking for a long time.

Turned out, it was the first.

"No fire to put out, just a crisis—a chocolate cake crisis, to be exact. I need you to come and taste my chocolate cake, and tell me if it's any good," she said. And added, "at your convenience. But today, if you can."

Colton sent back a *thumb's up* emoji and a *smiley face*. Chocolate cake was his favorite treat—he came by that honestly, from Ridge. But most of all, he was happy to think Liu might be making up an excuse to see him again. It sent a shiver up his spine, in spite of the warm day.

"She *likes* me," he said to himself, and stood a little taller.

But when he arrived at the cook's house, it really was the cake she needed help with.

Liu was standing behind the large workstation, looking uncharacteristically disheveled. She had a smear of cocoa powder on her cheek, and flour smudges on her normally pristine apron. In front of her stood what may or may not have been a cake, sitting on a pedestal.

"Kat asked me to prepare a special meal for your dad's birthday party in a few weeks," Liu said with a note of panic in her voice. "She said his favorite cake is chocolate. But I've only eaten my grandmother's chocolate cake, which I never really liked."

Colton sat down on one of the stools and scooted closer to the work surface. He had left his boots and hat by the door, and first went to wash his hands at the sink. Careful now not to dredge his shirt sleeve in the all-over baking debris, he picked up the fork Liu offered him, and dove it into the slice of cake set before him.

This *looked* like a chocolate cake, but it was dense, and had the faint aroma of vegetables.

As he put a bit in his mouth—with Liu watching him like a hawk—she said, "my grandmother hardly uses any sugar. She makes her cake with pureed beets, and arrowroot flour."

The gumminess and acrid flavor of the bite hit him hard, along with her words—like a double whammy. *Pow. Pow!*

He chewed and nodded diplomatically, trying to find the words to say to Chef Liu. There was nothing *cake-like* in the bite. If he had a blindfold on, he would swear the food in his mouth was a liver pate, or maybe turkey gravy that had seized up and hardened.

"Well?" Liu asked, with hope in her voice.

"Your grandmother," Colton started to say, as gently as he could, "she... calls this *cake?*"

Liu's shoulders slumped. "I knew it. It's bad, isn't it?"

Colton started to nod "yes" as a knee-jerk reaction, then immediately shook his head "no" because he didn't want to hurt her feelings. As a result, his head tumbled around like a bobble headed toy.

Wanting to reassure her as vehemently as he could, he said, "Liu, I love your cooking. We all love your cooking, you gotta know that."

And they did!

The Wests had been enjoying Liu's clever dipping sauces and her spicy seasonings. They all devoured her soups and stews, and dumplings. On these warmer days, her light refreshing slaws and stir fries were just as satisfying to the hard-working family as the heavier casseroles had been. Only they didn't weigh everyone down.

"I haven't had heartburn once since Liu came on board," Ridge said to the family.

"High praise indeed," Kat said under her breath, to a smiling Gunnar.

True to her own preferences, Liu focused more on her vegetable-based sides and rice, but her steaks were grilled to perfection, as were the chicken breasts and wings she loved to cook and slather with her light and tangy chutneys.

But desserts were not her forte, they all discovered. Instead, Liu would include a bowl of freshly cut watermelon, or tangerine slices— dragon fruit, if she could source it. All of which Doctor Kat wholeheartedly approved of.

"Western cakes, with sugar and dairy ingredients," Liu started to explain to Colton, "have never been part of our culture. Most Asians are lactose intolerant."

"Again," Colton said, trying not to wrinkle his nose, "new information."

Liu just looked so defeated standing in her beautiful kitchen, which now looked like a powdery chocolate bomb had exploded, that he longed to fix whatever was broken.

"I'll tell you what," he said, cheerfully, "why don't I help you clean up, and then I'll take you out to dinner to a place that serves the best burgers and chocolate cake within a hundred miles."

Liu regarded his words.

"Burgers?" She sounded skeptical.

"Or whatever you want for dinner," Colton said, "but save room for the cake—it's my dad's favorite."

"So it's dinner, and research," Liu said with a serious nod.

"Sure, research," Colton repeated, thinking he needed to up his game with Liu. She didn't seem to be getting the message that he wanted to take her on a date.

Liu nodded, and when she spoke, she sounded like her usual confident self again.

"You wipe off the worktop," she commanded, "I'll go change my clothes. Then we'll go and taste this cake your father likes."

"*After* we eat," Colton wanted to clarify. He was hungry after his day.

"Burger first," Liu nodded after a moment, as if agreeing to a contractual bullet point.

An hour later, Colton sat across from Liu in a booth at Cindy's Diner. He had devoured his burger, along with a platter of French fries and a side salad. Liu enjoyed her pan-fried perch and sauteed green beans—she picked at them at first, but then managed to eat every bite.

"Everything okay?" Cindy herself came to the booth to welcome her esteemed West family guest, and his friend. After introductions, Colton explained that they came to taste-test her famous chocolate cake.

Liu was pleased that Colton didn't divulge that she herself had failed miserably at this dish, and was planning to steal as much information as needed. But she didn't need to steal. Cindy offered to show Liu how it was made.

"Come on back, Liu," Cindy said. "We are mixing up a fresh cake for tomorrow. I'll get Colton a slice of today's cake and a cup of coffee."

With that, Liu disappeared with Cindy for half an hour, while

Colton sipped coffee and looked out the window. At last, he heard excited voices that could only be the chef and the restaurant owner. He got up from the booth to say his farewells to Cindy and the staff.

"Don't forget what I said," Cindy was telling Liu as the women embraced.

"I won't," Liu said.

"Let me guess," Colton said to Cindy. "You offered Liu a job."

"She can come run my kitchen anytime she gets tired of the West family," Cindy said with a laugh, "but no. I told her not to skimp on the sugar, or butter."

"It's too much!" Liu complained.

"It's perfect—don't change a thing," Cindy said with an admonishing smile.

CHAPTER 14

"Cindy really liked you," Colton exclaimed to Liu as they drove back to the ranch. The sun was dipping down behind the mountains and the air was cooling off as it did on summer nights. Colton went slow to avoid running into the mule deer and moose that came out at dusk to eat the tall grass.

"She likes *you*, and your family," Liu responded.

Colton was silent for a minute. Cindy had always been happy to see the Wests when anyone in the family came to eat. He also knew that his mother's foundation, the West Foundation, had helped Cindy and her staff get through the epidemic that forced them to close their doors shortly after Kat arrived in town. But he'd always thought being nice was just Cindy's way.

"Are you saying she only helped you because you were with me?"

Liu shrugged but didn't answer for a while.

"Colton," she said at last, "if I had walked in to Cindy's diner by myself and asked for her recipe for chocolate cake, do you think she would have been as gracious?"

"Well, maybe not," he said, "that's a tall order for a stranger. But if you said you were my friend, she probably would."

"Exactly," Liu said.

"I guess I'm not following you, Liu," Colton said. "That seems pretty normal for most people around here. We all help our friends, and we help our friends' friends too."

He pulled his Range Rover off the road at a scenic turnout, and asked Liu if she'd like to get out and enjoy the sunset with him. At her nod, the two followed a short path to a bench that overlooked the winding creek, and the foothills of the mountains.

As they sat, Colton silently pointed to a bull moose in the distance, eating the leaves of a bushy willow tree. Liu shook her head in wonder, and looked up at Colton. They shared a smile, and neither continued the conversation they'd begun earlier. Though Liu couldn't help but wonder how much her family's outlook on the world around them had affected her own perspective about strangers.

"Anyway Colton," Liu said softly, as she looked up at the young cowboy. He had such a kind face, she thought, as he turned to smile down at her. "Thank you for taking me to Cindy's tonight to taste the chocolate cake."

Colton's smile was so genuine, that in spite of her better judgment, Liu found herself lowering her natural defenses. "You dropped every-thing today just to help me out," she said with wonder in her eyes. "I've never had such a friend."

And it was true. Liu knew that contrary to the show of confidence she displayed for all the world to see, at times she had doubts, and fears, and insecurities about whether she could do all that she'd set out to. Yet having someone in her life like Colton West gave her courage. Knowing she could call on him for help and support was a new experience for Liu.

Her parents often talked about friendship as the foundation for their love and devotion to each other. "Your father is my close *friend*," Ling would emphasize about Zhang, and for years Liu had nodded as if she understood, then secretly rolled her eyes.

Young girls dreamed of falling in love, and being swept off their feet. Not finding a friend!

But she was starting to see a deeper significance.

Growing up, her American friendships would come and go each

school year, depending on the whims of silly girls and their new clothes, or new boyfriends. Now, Liu wondered if Ling was trying to tell her that romantic love can be fleeting, and to start with friendship.

Looking up, she gave Colton a smile. Declaring him to be a friend was a big deal in her culture—one he probably didn't understand. And it was new territory for her, too. If only she wasn't already on thin ice with her family, she might be more open to exploring a romantic relationship with Colton. But she knew it could never be.

As for Colton, he tried not to be disappointed at her choice of words. Especially when she gazed at him with such a radiant and genuine smile. With other women—American women—that kind of smile would be all the green light he'd need to move a little closer, and lean in for a kiss. He sensed that would be a misstep with Liu at this particular moment.

But "friend" seemed the complete opposite of what he was going for.

Their evening had been nice. Liu was so easy to talk to, and he enjoyed being with her.

Granted, Cindy's Diner wasn't the height of elegance when it came to fancy date locations, but she seemed to appreciate his good intentions—letting her experience the best example of chocolate cake in the area, since the poor girl had grown up thinking a slab of solidified beet puree was actually a dessert.

What if he stepped up his game, would she take the bait?

A few days later, Colton was ready to test the waters. Sending Liu a message, he asked if she'd like to join him for a picnic by the gorge. If so, he'd pick up a moveable feast from town, and come get her.

CHAPTER 15

*L*iu looked at Colton's message. Her index finger hovered above the letter N for "no" for an awfully long time. But two things kept her from turning him down.

The first reason was friendship. In her culture, when someone declares another to be a friend, it's taken seriously. If a friend asks something of you that you can fulfill, you do it. And there was no reason Liu couldn't join Colton for a picnic. She was exceeding deadlines and expectations for her cooking, and her evening was free.

The other reason was this new and strange tingling feeling she was starting to get when she was with Colton West. When she touched his hand, and when he sat next to her on the bench by the gorge—when they ate together at Cindy's diner. Even when he showed up at her door for a snack. She got a physical reaction that pleased her, and she wanted more of it.

Liu was drawn to the warmth of his scent. And the way he placed his hand lightly on her back whenever they walked through doors, or meadows. His fingertips left memories that both tormented and comforted her in the night. The way his eyes took her in made her feel as though she was something valuable that he was sworn to protect and defend—like pearls or precious gems in a palace.

When she saw his truck pull up to the cook house, Liu's stomach would burble up and her heart would pound until it was loud and deafening and wonderful.

But Liu also knew that once her family set a Chinese courtship in motion, she might never get another chance to experience these amazing feelings. She was playing with fire, and knew it. Yet Liu thought she could get one step closer before getting burned.

You can never be my husband!

"Yes," she messaged back.

COLTON SMILED to himself at the thought of spending the evening with Liu Chen and her beautiful almond eyes. He was determined to do all he could to dispel her notion that he was a nut, or just a friend. If his boyish charm got him in the door, great. But he had to find a new way to take next steps.

He went home for a shower and a clean shirt before picking her up —and when she opened the door wearing a flouncy blouse and a radiant smile, he knew he was on the right track. His grin must have betrayed his thoughts, and she called him on it.

"What?!" Liu wanted to know, looking down to see what Colton saw.

"Nothing," he shrugged, smiling even broader. "You look pretty, that's all."

She wasn't convinced, he could tell, but he held out his hand and she took it.

The afternoon had been warm, so he drove down a little-travelled two-track on the ranch to a small creek that flowed gently over a few large, flat boulders. It was the perfect park on their property, with nothing but untouched land as far as they eye could see.

"I brought a quilt to spread on the shore for the picnic," Colton said after getting out of the Jeep, "but before we eat, beautiful lady, there's some business you and I need to take care of."

Liu melted a little at his words, and watched his face as he spoke. She had no idea what he had in mind, but decided to follow his lead.

Holding her gaze, Colton took his hat off and hung it on a tree limb. Liu did the same with her sunhat. Next, he took off one boot, then another.

Liu slipped off one sandal, then another, without breaking eye contact.

The way he was looking at her sent a shiver up her spine that made no sense, Liu thought, in light of the weather. And she hoped this was as far as Colton's striptease was going. She only had a few items of clothing left.

With a private smile, Colton then bent down and rolled up the pantleg of his jeans, halfway to his knees. He reached out and held his hand out for Liu, who watched every move.

"Colton, I," Liu hesitated, looking at his hand. She didn't always know how to read American body language, but was certain he had something specific in mind.

Was she ready?

"Trust me, Liu," he said, and surprisingly, Liu found that she did. She reached up and gave him her hand, and he nodded with satisfaction. They stood very still for a moment, before he gave her hand a little tug.

Minutes later, they were laughing and sitting side by side on the flat rock, with their feet soaking in the cool rushing water.

"Ahh, that's very nice," Liu exhaled with delight at the sensation.

"What did I tell you?" Colton said. The water felt so good, as did Liu's bare shoulder, pressed against his summer shirt. Liu and Colton, in turns, looked from the bottom of the clear blue stream to the tops of the tall mountain peaks before them. They listened to the water rushing over stones, and the breeze rattle the Aspen trees.

With their backs each supporting the other, Colton and Liu turned their faces to the lowering sun to absorb the warm rays. When they both said they were hungry, Colton stood up in the stream and turned towards Liu with his arms out.

"You don't want to put those pretty feet on the ground," he said with a smile. Moments later, she was in his arms as he carried her to the picnic. She laughed in surprise, but easily draped her arms around his neck as he enjoyed the feel of her smooth legs.

"Now I wish I hadn't put the blanket so near," he said, reluctantly setting her down and removing his hands from her warm skin.

Soon, they were stretched out and unpacking the basket.

"Nice job, Colton," Liu said. "Berries, and shrimp, and cold skirt steak," Liu exclaimed with delight, pulling out food and forks. Colton poured chilled sparkling cider and lifted his glass to hers for a toast.

"To Chef Liu Chen," he said. "May you have many years of happiness at West Ranch."

"How could I not?" Liu said as she lifted her glass.

A shadow passed her thoughts just then. A dark shadow filled with many ways she could definitely not be happy—by being with another man on Colton's ranch, for instance. Or seeing Colton with someone else. But she pushed the shadow away and took a sip of the cold and bubbly drink.

Colton and Liu watched the sun dip down over the hills as they ate and drank. They laughed together over Liu's grandmother's cake, and talked about Colton's housing development. They shared stories from their childhoods, and family anecdotes.

Liu was very at ease, and found herself sitting very close to Colton on the quilt as he leaned back on one arm; legs fully stretched out. She was drawn to his smile and his expressive hands, and the way his eyes scrunched up and sparkled when he teased her.

She liked who she was when she was with him. She didn't feel like someone who need to try harder or work smarter or faster, or be better. This was another new feeling—being just fine the way she was.

A lull in the conversation caused Colton to sit up on the quilt, bringing his face just inches from her own. Neither one moved away.

Colton held her gaze. His smile faded just a small bit, and his eyes grew serious.

"Well look at this," he practically whispered to Liu, "a little leaf wanted to be in your silky hair. Can't say I blame it."

Bringing one hand tentatively near her shoulder, he tenderly took a lock of her jet-black hair between his finger and thumb and lightly caressed it. It was an intimate gesture. He knew from experience that she would either pull away, or let him come closer. Seeing that she didn't pull away, Colton tenderly continued to enjoy the way the silkiness of her hair felt between his fingers, as it tickled his hand.

With his eyes, he followed the tips down to where her hair rested on her tanned shoulder. Colton longed to run his fingers down the bare skin of her arm, but didn't want to startle her. She was mesmerized by him, he could tell.

Leaning in for a kiss would have been a natural next step.

But something happened inside Colton just then, and he froze. He realized he'd come to the absolute end of everything he thought he knew about women, and kissing. This wasn't just any woman, and this wouldn't be just any kiss.

This was... *her.*

A voice inside said, *Stop, this is as far as you go. It's up to Liu.*

He waited on pins and needles forever, it seemed, to see if she'd move closer to him or not. Colton was spellbound by her deep dark almond eyes and the way her long eyelashes fluttered.

She smelled like vanilla, and exotic flowers, and everything good.

When she did move closer—just an inch or two—Colton felt ridiculously happy and a little reckless, but held his position with great control. The only move he made was to tilt his head.

He was close enough to feel her sweet breath on his face. He smiled just a little, hearing her breathing become faster with anticipation. Liu tipped her head the opposite way, and brought her lips so close to his—and stopped, while she searched his eyes.

Oh please oh please, find what you're looking for, his heart silently cried.

His whole body tingled at the thought of kissing Liu, just moments away. And when her full lips parted ever so slightly, the tingling turned to anticipation that was almost painful in its pleasure. At last, her eyelids fluttered again, and her lips met his own.

Hers were like velvet in their softness, yet she leaned into him decisively.

Colton moved a free hand behind Liu's back, and pulled her gently towards him as their lips remained softly upon the others. Thousands of nerve endings seemed to come alive for Colton as she leaned into his kiss.

This is it, Colton thought, mid-kiss. This is what he'd longed to do since she first caught him in her shower, weeks before. He tried to pull his mind away from the memory of that moment—he was getting way ahead of himself.

Finally, Colton gently moved back and opened his eyes. Liu did the same. Then he took her hand in his own.

"That was amazing," Colton said.

"That was a mistake," Liu declared at the same time, while standing up and gathering the basket in her hand.

"*What...* but... I want you to be my girlfriend," he stumbled over his words in surprise.

"Girlfriend?" Liu turned back to face him. "I am too old to be the girlfriend of a cowboy. It's time for me to be a wife, in a Chinese marriage."

"I thought you were joking," Colton said.

"No," Liu said, with sadness in her voice.

She should never have allowed that kiss to happen. She'd only been on the ranch for a month, and by becoming entangled with the family this way, she was putting everything at risk. Her job, her reputation, and the trust her family had in her.

How had she gotten caught up in Colton West? He was like one of those dust tornadoes on the prairie that whirled along until it was stopped in its tracks—and she had to be the one to stop him. She would have to dig deep and be the no-nonsense Liu Chen that set clear boundaries, even if it hurt him.

"That was a nice kiss Colton. A very tasty bite," she said in a clipped voice. "But you and I can never be more than friends."

She turned and purposefully walked away.

"It's impossible."

CHAPTER 16

*H*er clipped rejection felt like a punch in the stomach.

Speechless, Colton watched as Liu sauntered beautifully to his Range Rover in her flowery shirt, wearing strappy sandals that showed off her delicate feet and painted toenails. She looked good. She smelled good. And while Colton wasn't a rocket scientist, he would swear she had dressed up for him and their picnic.

Had he misjudged her desire to kiss him? Colton didn't think so. And yet, she flippantly brushed him off, saying they could never be more than friends.

And it hurt!

Colton took his first reluctant steps towards the truck. There was nothing to do but take her home, and lick his wounds. But kissing Liu Chen had changed him, and he couldn't forget that. When he held her in his arms, he felt like he was holding his future; his *grown-up life*.

For such a tiny thing, she had captivated his heart and his thoughts. But contrary to the message her kiss sent to his body and soul, she claimed they couldn't be together. And he didn't think he knew how to combat her no-nonsense ways.

Liu scared the big cowboy just a bit, truth be told.

. . .

ON THEIR WAY back to the ranch, Liu Chen gazed out the window of Colton's SUV. She admired the scenery—the sage brush and the hills were lined with aspen trees and evergreens. The road had been carved out long ago to follow the winding creek, occasionally crossing over it with a narrow bridge. As a result, it was common to spot wildlife in the dusk such as mule deer, moose, and later in the summer, the early migrating antelope.

She knew Colton was taking his time because of the animals near the road, but wondered if his slow speed matched the wind being taken out of his sails—by her.

Liu enjoyed kissing Colton West, and it was more intoxicating than she dreamt it would be. And she had dreamt of his kiss, ever since stumbling upon him installing her new shower fixture. She smiled to herself at catching the tall handsome cowboy in a vulnerable position, and how cute and frazzled he had been.

She suspected there weren't many times when Colton felt in over his head, and she prided herself on being one of them.

But there was no way her family would accept Colton.

Would they?

He was wealthy enough, that was for sure. But she didn't need money—her family was doing more than fine. For the Chens, honor was far more important than money.

The extended multi-generation family had raised her to understand her place in the group, and the expectations they had for her. They took care of each other, and one person's decision affected everyone under the Chen roof.

As a small girl, when her great grandmother was still alive but failing in health, everyone calibrated their lives to care for her needs, and show her great respect in her final days. She was never an inconvenience, as some of her non-Asian friends made their grandparents out to be—she was never sent to a nursing home only to be visited on weekends and holidays.

And when Liu decided on culinary school, she consulted with each member of her family during elaborate tea ceremonies, having in-depth discussions with each. Only when she had everyone's blessing—

when everyone told her in turn that "culinary school was favorable"—did she proceed.

They were proud of her, she knew. But even though she had moved to the cook house of the West Ranch, she was not removed from the family structure. There was still a golden strand of heritage and expectation connecting her to the greater Chen household. Someday, she would marry a fellow Chinese, they had instilled in her. And the couple would either move back with the Chens, or the Chens would move in with her to care for the household and the children.

How to tell Colton all this? How could she boil down centuries of her family history for him in a way that he'd understand?

Liu ventured a glance at Colton as he drove. He looked sad, and in spite of her hard demeanor, his defeat tugged at her heart. She really liked him. He was attentive and interested, and she was aware that his easy-going ways left plenty of room for her own abrupt opinions and mannerisms to shine.

She smiled at the way he wasn't put out when she barked her quiet orders, or commanded him to "sit" by pointing her knife. Just the opposite—he seemed to draw closer to her. And yet, she needed to be careful not to treat Colton like somebody she could push around.

But the few times she'd kissed a man, it was not a big deal. She expected it to be the same with Colton. Surprisingly, though, when Colton held her in his strong arms, she could feel her defenses melting to the edges like gooey white chocolate bits in a double boiler.

Colton's warm and musky aroma was unlike anything she'd ever inhaled before. It seemed to have invisible fingers that unlocked her tight countenance, disarming her and drawing her closer to him.

Stirring her.

Her sense of taste was also heightened when his warm lips touched her own. She never did have a sweet tooth, but that was okay. Colton's kiss tasted buttery and savory, like a delicacy she could never get enough of.

But it was his strong arms that wrapped firmly around her slight back that she could feel, even now, riding in the truck. He pulled her closer to him so gently, but like a man who would be strong when she needed him to be.

Liu herself was tough. She had to be. As an Asian chef in the wild west, she was small. And her cooking went against the grain of the usual *cattle country* preferences. But it was nice to know that if she needed to let her guard down and allow someone to be strong on her behalf, Colton West was her man.

With this in mind, Liu saw his right arm draping casually on the center arm rest, and slowly moved her hand to gently touch his own. Instinctively, his fingers entwined hers as his head turned her way with a glimmer of optimism and unasked questions.

Turning her gaze to face the front, she silently let him know that there would be no answers that night. Only the slight hope of her hand resting in his.

CHAPTER 17

"Finally," Ridge said triumphantly to his computer screen.

With his confirmation email from the registry office of Land and Deeds, he could soon make a formal bid on the Madison bungalow in town—the little house next door to the one Ash had inherited from his grandmother. Just as soon as they started the bidding, in days.

Keeping his plan to himself, Ridge was hoping to buy the little property, and then work alongside Ash as they both renovated their homes. His goal was two-fold. First, he would be able to tighten his bond with Ash over trips to the hardware store and lumber yard. Eventually, the two would have side-by-side rental homes in West Gorge and help each other out. Like business partners.

Also, Ash's project should go a long way in keeping the young man out of trouble. He'd be too occupied with his plans for the bungalow—on top of his school work—to get the itch to lift things that weren't his.

Ash acting out didn't concern Ridge lately. Once the adoption had been finalized, he felt the boy exhale and relax more fully than he had before. Ash was a true West now, surrounded by family who would support him and keep him on the straight and narrow.

And for the first time in a long while, Ridge felt like he was getting back to his roots in some way—by improving the little town named after his grandfather, and by *acquiring*. He was genuinely *excited* about something.

For many years, the Wests scooped up parcels of land by the armful, anytime it was available. They sacrificed many luxuries in the early years in order to be cash-ready to increase their holdings, and it had paid off. What the Wests didn't need for their own ranching needs they leased to other ranchers; to oil wells, to industrial developers and manufacturers.

Now, the Wests owned industrial complexes, grazing and hunting lands, and retail properties. They owned the fancy new housing development in town: West Gorge Woods. And of course, they owned a goodly chunk of Wyoming with the sprawling ranch.

But it was the unassuming little downtown bungalow that was on Ridge's radar. The thought of owning that little mite of a house got Ridge to feeling his wild oats once again. He wanted to conquer that house, and prove to himself—and that upstart realtor, Casey Parks—that old Ridge West was still a force to be reckoned with.

Shadows of old sensations began coursing through his veins, ones he thought were long dormant. It could only be the thrill of the hunt —and the win. He was going to *win* that little house, for himself and his son.

"No, you can't go in the house, Ridge," Patricia told him on the phone the next day. "Same as everyone else. It's a blind auction."

"What fool would buy a house sight unseen?" He challenged her.

"I guess we'll find out," Patricia laughed.

"Aw, seriously, Patricia…" Ridge started to press a little heavier on the pedal.

"Seriously *yourself*, Ridge West," she said. "You never did like following the rules, but I didn't make this rule—the bank did. Just like other folks, you can read the specs online and see a few pictures. *Unlike* other folks, you can afford a million little bungalows, without feeling a pinch in your wallet. So let's not have any more rubbish."

"Mmm," Ridge grumbled. He knew Patricia was right. But it was the principle of the thing that bothered him. Still, the sellers were smart. Better for top dollar to shield the truth from the buyers, and let them find out after the sale just what they got for their money.

"It's your own fault, Ridge," Patricia went on. "This once-small town is getting too big for its britches. Casey Parks and other realtors will be happy to scoop it up at any price, then renovate it before the aspen trees turn yellow."

Casey Parks.

He'd never seen Casey Parks, but her name kept popping up to where she was becoming a thorn in his side. He'd show her and rest of 'em, though. These rental house owners didn't know who they were up against, now that he was tossing his cowboy hat in the ring.

"I guess it's fair, as long as Casey Parks isn't getting a look either," Ridge said.

"Nope, it's all fair and square," she said before hanging up.

But Ridge smiled, knowing he had a secret advantage come auction day—the bidding would start at midnight on his *birthday.* Surely there would be good luck in that.

CHAPTER 18

"With just the family we'll have about ten people," Kat told Liu. They were sitting at Liu's table, drinking green tea and talking about Ridge's birthday party. It was mid-morning, when little Willow was taking her first nap of the day after rising early.

"Ten family members?" Liu asked, wondering if there was someone she hadn't yet met.

"Oh, right," Kat said, "I didn't tell you that a few cousins are coming down from Montana for the party—Gunnar calls them the *north* Wests."

Liu smiled at the wordplay.

"Rowdy is a retired rodeo rider, and his brother Gray is a pilot. He fights the wildfires that seem to break out every September in the forests and mountains," Kat said. "They'll be staying in the guest house for a week or so."

Liu nodded, and wrote their names down on her pad of paper. She would have to factor in two more ravenous cowboys into the West family menu.

"And then with a handful of friends from town," Kat said, "we might have 35 or 40 guests for the party. I expect Colton might bring a date..."

Liu choked on her tea and had to catch herself. She turned away from Kat.

"You okay?" Kat asked her chef.

"Fine… fine," Liu got up and took a sip of water. "You think Colton… might bring a *date?*"

Liu was caught off guard, mostly by the surge of jealousy she felt at Kat's comment. Who could Colton possibly bring to his dad's party, when he had been kissing *her* the other night?

Leaning against the kitchen counter, Liu looked out the window to where Colton had insisted on walking her to her door after their picnic, even after she told him they could never be more than friends. That his interest in her had been reignited was no one's fault but her own—she's the one who took his hand while they were riding home.

And as for their second and more passionate kiss, she'd like to blame Wyoming and its warm summer breezes. But she had to own that one too.

Liu's legs felt weak all over again when she thought of it.

THEY WERE STANDING on her porch—Colton had insisted on walking her to her door. Turning to thank him for their picnic, Liu found herself dangerously close to his warm scent and beating heart. As a summer breeze moved a few clouds over the stars in the vast Wyoming sky, she inhaled deeply, breathing in both the night air and the intoxicating cowboy on her threshold.

She didn't mean to place her tiny hand on his chest, but before she knew it, she was touching Colton and looking up to see what his eyes had in store for her.

Everything, as it turned out.

She saw deep longing, and the way Colton was vulnerable in spite of his stature. But he was not a man to take charge of. With Colton West, she found herself craving the opposite.

Liu was about to send him away again, and remind Colton that they could never fall in love with each other; that they had no future together. But the longing in his eyes, and his slightly parted lips did her in. Just an hour before, those lips had been pressed against hers as they sat by the creek. As the water splashed into the rocks, she had felt her body and soul splashing and leaning into the rock that was Colton West.

With that memory at the forefront of her mind, Liu stretched her arms up and around Colton's neck as he stood on her porch, and urgently drew herself towards him once again.

He responded by wrapping his own arms around her and pulling her up until their lips met. Their goodnight kiss was more passionate than the tender creek-side kiss had been, making it harder than ever to convince Colton they couldn't be together.

"Liu?" It was Kat's voice, pulling her back to the party planning. "Should we call Red, or another caterer to cook for the birthday party guests, do you think? I don't expect you to always serve our larger crowds on your own."

Whether Kat intended her comment to have the result it did or not, Liu snapped back to the present with a vengeance. The ambitious chef had considered it an epic fail that her first event, Granny's funeral, had to be catered because she had just arrived.

"Absolutely not," Liu declared to Kat. "I've got this!"

Kat and Liu continued to discuss the details. Kat told the chef that weather permitting, they could hold the festivities at the ranch pavilion. A vendor was coming in the day before to string lights, and decorate. "So that's one thing we don't have to worry about," she said.

Gunnar arranged for a small band to play, and Ash had a few friends from school who would be happy to earn a few dollars. They would park cars for the guests, and help Liu's staff with whatever running she needed.

"Paislee wants to help," Kat said, "so she's overseeing the decorations and invitations."

Liu nodded, trying not to think about Colton and his mysterious date.

"Oh..." Kat said, "what about a cake? Should we order one from the bakery?"

Kat knew when she hired Liu that baking was not her forte, and was fine with it. In her opinion, there had been way too many treats for the men of West Ranch in the past thirty years. She herself enjoyed a cookie or two, but the men had been spoiled, the doctor thought. And each cowboy could stand to lose a pound or two.

Not to mention, they needed to give their arteries a fighting chance. Liu's fresh dishes were much healthier than the sugar, white flour, and cheese that had been coursing through the veins of the Wests these past thirty years.

Kat loved the retired cook—they all did. But as Gunnar had said more than once, "there was a new sheriff in town," and Kat wasn't shy about letting her voice be heard at the ranch. With Chef Liu, the family enjoyed bowls of fruit for dessert, in place of the heavier cakes and pies.

"I'd like to try and make the cake," Liu said, pulling Kat back from her own wandering thoughts. "Colton took me to Cindy's Diner for a slice of their chocolate cake. He said it was Ridge's favorite."

"Oh?"

Kat's ears tingled as she tried to read between the lines. After all, the good doctor didn't become an expert in infectious diseases by ignoring small details, and how they interconnected. She was used to looking at life through a microscope, and this conversation was no different.

First, Liu choked on her tea at the mention of Colton bringing a girl to the party.

Then Liu admitted that she and Colton have been spending time together, eating out. He took the beautiful and trendy young chef up to Cindy's for dinner and dessert.

That sounded a lot like a *date* to Kat, which raised more than one red flag.

But Kat smiled and nodded at Liu as they wrapped up their meeting, each agreeing to revisit the cake decision after Liu had a few days to try her hand at the chocolate confection.

Minutes later, foot hard on the accelerator, she aimed her car for the big house, and came to a screeching halt very close to the front. Not taking the time to park in the garage, as usual.

Stomping heavily, Kat stormed through the front door and into the kitchen, where Gunnar and Colton, she knew, would be having breakfast. Both men sat up straighter at the sound of Kat and looked at each other in alarm.

Who's in trouble? They both wondered.

"Colton," Kat said, answering their silent question to Gunnar's great relief. She sounded sharp and annoyed.

"Kat?" Colton looked up in innocent surprise at her tone.

"How long have you been kissing the cook?"

CHAPTER 19

*T*wo days later, Colton sat outside looking like a lost puppy without a boy. He took a bite of the cold sandwich he'd picked up at the deli in town. Next to him, on the picnic table by the site where he planned on building his house, sat a cooling cup of coffee.

Colton looked over at the stakes, eyeing the layout of the floorplan as he ate his lunch. He'd like a big family someday, and longed for a large kitchen to match—filled with pantries, and cookies, and someone like Liu preparing tantalizing stews and delectable dishes. Maybe someone exactly like Liu.

He smiled at the thought.

Taking another bite, he looked up at the mountains and down at the creek. This was the one place he came to when wanted to be alone, which would surprise his family. His brothers and his dad didn't think he ever wanted to be alone.

"A *people person*," his mother used to call him with a broad grin.

He would always be a *people person* when it came to Randi West— she was his all-time favorite person in the world, before she died from the cancer. On that day, Gunnar ran off to spend time in the hills. Pike took off for the ancient barn on the other side of the property, to paint, they now knew.

Ridge stayed in his room and sobbed—they could hear his cries throughout the massive house, though he tried to stifle them.

As for Colton, who would have welcomed the presence and consolation of his family, he made his way over to the creek and cried his heart out all by himself. Right here, on the spot he wanted to build his house.

"Mama, I sure do miss you now," Colton said to the soft July wind. He had always been able to share his heart with his mother, and no matter how busy she was with the ranch or the foundation, she was all ears for her youngest boy.

"Colton West," she'd say to him through her smiles, "you are just a sparkler and a firecracker—you light up the sky and my whole world, each and every day."

Since kissing Liu Chen, Colton was beginning to understand how life could be lit up by somebody else. He didn't realize that he'd been so lonely until meeting Liu. Now, all he wanted to do was be near her, and with her.

He explained all this to Kat two days earlier, when she had been upset with him. And rightly so, he had reluctantly agreed. Once he heard her reasoning against the relationship, that is.

"She's an employee of West Ranch, Colton," Kat tried to tell him. "There's a huge conflict of interest here."

"But I might be falling in love with her, Kat," Colton said, helplessly.

Kat softened quickly, no longer angry with her younger brother-in-law, but compassionate towards his tender heart and loneliness.

"Besides," he told her. "I'm not an employee of West Ranch. West Development is its own separate entity. I just live here… and eat here."

"You *own* the ranch," Kat pointed out, "same as Gunnar, Pike, and Ash." And little Willow, Kat thought to herself.

"I reckon," he said, deflated.

"Just please tread carefully," Kat admonished.

And with that conversation, she was immediately conflicted. She longed with all her heart for Colton to find love and happiness with a young woman who would appreciate his fine qualities. A woman just like Liu.

But she didn't want to lose her—Liu was a talented chef; a rare find amidst the hash-slingers and bean scoopers of the great American West.

And somewhere in the middle, she knew, there was an unspeakable scenario where Liu could claim she felt pressured to have a romantic relationship in order to keep her job. The fallout, even if skewed and untrue, could be devastating to the West's good name—and to the reputation they've had in the community for 150 years.

COLTON DECIDED to lay low for a few days, and not eat with the family. He left early to get his breakfast at a drive-thru in town, and then went back again for a deli sandwich. But he missed seeing Liu at the ranch, and he missed sitting in her kitchen and being fed all sorts of dumplings, and skewers, and salads. He missed his mouth burning up from her spicy sauces. And missed the taste of her sweet kiss.

Colton warmed at the thought of her lips, and her hands wrapped around his neck.

Liu had objections to dating an American, he knew, because of her family. How could he show her—and them—that he was willing to learn their customs, and their heritage? Colton wanted to go see Liu at the cook house, but noticed another car parked there. Kat mentioned that her grandparents and mother had come to stay for a few days. They were going to help Liu prepare the food for Ridge's birthday party.

At the mention of their visit, his first instinct was to go and say hello, but Kat slowed him down. "Wait until you're invited," she suggested.

Dang.

He wanted more than anything to march in and tell the Chens that he didn't care if they didn't approve. He was going to date Liu anyway, whether they liked it or not. But Kat was wise. That was a very heavy-handed response, he could see. And more like a temper tantrum. It was not a move that would endear the more controlled Liu to him as a suitor.

Something he hated to admit even to himself, but had to, was that he was afraid of being disliked by the Chen family—or by anybody. He'd never experienced that in his young life, and wasn't sure he could handle it. Especially without his mother to see him through the rough patches. There was nobody else he could share his feelings with.

Maybe Kat.

But not Ridge, or his brothers. These rough and tumble cowboys were set in their ways, and not used to talking about "feelings." At least with Colton.

As he gazed around at the land where he had chosen to build his family home, feeling stronger at the memory of his mother's own strength, he decided then and there that—God willing—it was Liu who would share it with him.

CHAPTER 20

"My daughter tells me you have made her very welcome at West Ranch," Ling Chen nodded and smiled at Kat and Paislee. The West women sat in the kitchen of the cook house, tucking pork filling into dumpling rounds and pinching the ends together—under the watchful eye and helpful hands of Ling, as well as Liu's grandmother Chun.

Kat and Paislee couldn't resist the invitation by Liu to join the Chens, and learn to make the traditional Chinese dish. The five women sat companionably on stools around the large island.

"Liu is a gift to our family, Mrs. Chen," Kat responded with a slight bow of her head. "She works hard, and everyone is delighted with her meals."

"Even the men," Paislee chimed in with a smile.

Once again, Kat thanked Ling for inviting them to the cooking lesson. The dumplings would be served at Ridge's birthday party, so she and Paislee were doubly glad to be included in the preparations.

"Many hands," Ling said with her soft, graceful mannerisms, "make for light work."

Kat and Paislee nodded once again—Kat in her blouse; Paislee in her prairie dress. Both were trying hard to mirror the etiquette of the

Chens, and were nervous at the thought of doing something wrong. Or bringing bad luck. But their fears quickly left at the warm welcome.

Liu's mother Ling seemed just as contemporary as her daughter. She was dressed elegantly, yet practically for a day of cooking. Ling nodded often to her mother, and translated for Chun when necessary.

"We appreciate that you invited us to make dumplings for the birthday party," Kat said. "These delicacies are so flavorful, but certainly take skill."

"We are glad you think our dumplings are delicacies," Ling said with a smile. "In our culture, they are an everyday food."

"It's true," Liu chimed in. "This was my after-school snack."

Chun sat between Kat and Paislee and often reached over to correct their amount of stuffing, or their pinching technique. Kat was of the opinion that Chun understood everything they were saying, but wasn't as confident in her English speaking.

After a while, Chun excused herself to go make tea for the women. After putting the water on, Kat heard Willow fuss from the car carrier she was napping in. She made a move to check on her, but Chun said "no, no," to Kat, and scurried happily to get the baby.

Ling also stopped what she was doing and rushed over to Willow.

Then the grandfather appeared out of nowhere. Willow looked up from her sleep to see three eager and smiling faces staring at her expectantly. She let out a small cry, only to be met with three adults talking to her, tickling her toes, and shaking her rattles.

Ling scooped the baby up, and the grandparents followed Ling and the baby to the guestroom, the three cooing and chattering in melodic Chinese baby speak as they went.

Kat looked up at Liu with a question on her face.

"How many Chinese grandparents does it take to change a diaper?" Liu asked Kat and Paislee with a small laugh. "The answer is simple, every single one of them! They *love* babies. Willow is in good hands, Kat. My family is waiting anxiously for a grandchild of their own."

Kat relaxed and smiled.

"No pressure there," Paislee said, with a slight note of sarcasm. "I understand though. Pepper and Drake Andrews are chomping at the bit for Pike and I to produce the next in line."

Kat looked at Paislee with compassion, and reached over to her sister-in-law. "You and Pike haven't been married a year," Kat said. "Don't put that on yourself, Paislee."

Paislee smiled back. "I know. My *head* knows, anyway. But when I see Willow…"

"Well Auntie Paislee," Kat said, trying to lighten the mood, "anytime you want a baby fix, just say the word. It's been hard to find a nanny, and I'm not ready to hand her to just any sitter."

Paislee smiled in return, then looked at Liu. "Are you dating anyone?"

At the question, Kat looked down at her dumpling, trying not to make eye contact with Liu. She didn't want to give herself away as someone who knew she was seeing Colton.

"Not really," Liu answered casually, "nothing serious."

Kat's eyes flew off of the dumpling and onto the chef. Suddenly, her thoughts of protecting Liu from Colton flip-flopped—was Liu toying with Colton's heart? She wasn't sure who she should be looking out for. If she asked Gunnar, he'd be sure to say, "stay out of it, Kat. You don't need to look out for anyone but me and Willow."

When Willow came into the kitchen, Kat expected her to reach for mama from Ling's arms, but that did not happen. The baby looked quite content, and Kat just observed as she moved peacefully to the grandfather's happy arms while Ling gathered a quick lunch for Willow, and Chun went back to making tea.

Kat was mesmerized.

The Chens were like a well-oiled machine when it came to Willow. It was as if they really had been waiting for her to come along. The scenario was so unlike her own upbringing; her father couldn't seem to get away fast enough from their little family.

In minutes, Willow was sitting on a corner of the island being fed soft dumplings and bites of watermelon with wooden chopsticks. When the baby's attention would wander, Ling would gently say, "oi

Willow... *oi*" and the little one would eat another bite and smile, kicking her legs against the stainless work surface.

Chun set cups of tea in front of Kat and Paislee, then a different tea in front of Liu. All three women thanked Chun, who then went to join the baby feeding party, adding her smile to that of Ling and the grandfather.

After a few more bites, the foursome moved into the living room where they could sit on the floor and play with Willow and her toys.

Kat's mouth was still hanging open in surprise, she realized, and she picked up her tea to take a sip. "Ooh that's good, but yours looks different, Liu."

Liu rolled her eyes as she took a sip, then gave a small laugh.

"You and Paislee have a fertility tea," Liu said, "mine is a tea meant to help me find love."

Just then, the three women heard a truck pull into the cook house parking lot. A voice that sounded like Colton shouted, "is anybody home?"

Liu set down her cup and rushed out the door.

"Wow," Kat raised her eyebrows and said to Paislee, "that's some powerful tea."

CHAPTER 21

*L*iu was in the kitchen with Kat and Paislee, when to her horror she saw Colton's large truck pull up in the driveway, beyond the front porch and the other cars.

"What the… what is he…" Liu said under her breath, in a panic.

Why would Colton come unannounced while her family was with her?

It was good that her grandfather had come in from the porch. She could imagine big over-friendly Colton pouncing upon her small wiry grandfather with his usual cowboy exuberance.

Her grandfather spoke English when it suited him, but was a very quiet and gentle soul. Liu wasn't sure how he would react to Colton's larger-than-life personality. But if and when they did meet, she wanted to ease her family into the cowboy.

Now she was scrambling like an egg in a hot pan.

Liu's father was on a business trip, thank goodness, and not here to scrutinize Colton—who she knew wasn't going to turn around and go home without the introductions he came for.

Liu dashed towards the door after first untying her apron and throwing it on the island. She was only glad her family was preoccupied with Willow. Otherwise they would probably follow her outside, and complicate her intervention.

"Colton, hello," Liu said, fast-walking to Colton's truck as he got out.

"Liu," he said formally, with a nod and a smile, "I came to welcome your family."

Colton turned towards the truck and pulled out a box. When he turned around, Liu had her arms out like a defensive basketball player, trying to block him from stepping any closer to the house—if blocking him was even possible.

Amused, Colton smiled at her.

"Is there any way," she started to say, "that I can talk you out of this?"

"Why would you even want to do that, Liu?" Colton asked, truly surprised. "I waited a few days like Kat suggested, but around here, it's just bad manners not to say hello to new folks on the ranch."

Liu didn't think she was going to throw the cowboy off the scent of meeting her family, so she kicked into "damage control" mode before he could go marching towards the door.

"Okay, okay," Liu said nervously, "first things first. You can't wear that black shirt into the house—what are you wearing under it?"

Colton grinned with a mischievous smile. "You know better than anyone, Liu," he teased, referencing, she was certain, their first meeting in the steamy shower.

Liu struggled to hold onto her composure.

"This is not the time for your jokes. Do I see a yellow tee shirt folded on your back seat? Yellow is good—it's the *Yin and Yang* of the earth; the center of everything," Liu said, talking while her hands gestured. "Black is bad luck—it's *Hei*. You do not want my grandmother to judge you on the shirt."

With a shrug, Colton walked around to the other side of the truck while Liu followed. There they would both be hidden from any prying eyes. He took his hat off, and then worked the black tee shirt up and over his head. When he looked down, he saw that Liu couldn't take her eyes off of him, and he smiled at her.

"You like me, don't you?" He asked her, standing shirtless in front of her.

Liu shook her head to break the spell. "Don't be ridiculous, Colton, *please* put your shirt on."

"I will if you give me a kiss," he said with a mischievous smile.

"Are you *kidding*?" She asked in a panic. "My family is right in that house."

"They can't see us behind this tall truck," he said. "One kiss, then I'll put on the yellow shirt."

In spite of her frustration with the cowboy, Liu flashed him a smile, then stood on her tip toes to reach his lips. Not wanting just a friendly peck, Colton gently placed his hands on her shoulders to slow her down, then caught and held her attention with his eyes.

Liu's defenses melted at his touch. It seemed his gentleness was the kryptonite to her bossy, determined ways. She slowed her movements, until she was leaning up into his warm summer kiss like they had all the time in the world.

"Thank you," Colton said softly. "I've missed you."

"Now the shirt," Liu whispered back, trying to regain her no-nonsense voice.

Colton held her gaze as he threw on the clean West Development Co. tee he always kept in the car for meetings with customers or vendors.

"What's in the box?" Liu was anxious again when he came back around to grab his gift.

"A present for your family—four fresh pears and a pearl-handled fruit knife," Colton said proudly. "I ordered them special and they just arrived this morning."

Liu groaned loudly.

"Sorry, but you can't bring pears as a gift, Colton," Liu said, "the word *pears* is too close to the Chinese word for *parting*. And knives… no, no, no. Knives sever relationships!"

"You're pulling my leg," Colton sounded deflated as he placed the box back in the car.

"And never give gifts in multiples of four…" she said.

"Let me guess," Colton said, with defeat in his voice. "It's bad luck."

Liu's shoulders slumped as she faced Colton. "I know it's crazy, but if you want us to have a fighting chance, Colton, just go along with me."

Colton softened at her words, and reached out to take her in his arms. Immediately, Liu pulled away. "Just a few more things, and I'll introduce you."

"Okay, let me have it," he said, resigned.

"Don't touch or hug me, or them. Don't slap my grandfather on the back. Don't whistle, it's rude. Try not to make eye contact. Remember your open hands," she said, gesturing as a reminder of their conversation during their lunch by the creek.

"Is that all?" Colton's head was swimming.

"And please... please don't mention that we went out on a date, and kissed."

Colton caught Liu's eyes at the mention of their kisses.

"More than once," he drawled in a low voice, moving towards her so incrementally that only she would notice, should anyone be looking out the window.

Liu's cheeks burned as he spoke of her kisses with Colton, and their sweet embrace.

What was she doing, anyway? This relationship could never work, Liu thought to herself, miserably. She was only bringing conflict into her family by introducing them to Colton. And, she could be jeopardizing her new position by dating a member of the family, she knew.

Yet with all her reservations, here was Colton West, literally oozing with good will, good intentions, and his good nature. She may never meet another man quite like him in her lifetime.

Liu exhaled a deep, resigned breath, gesturing to Colton to come with her to the little house. Where, she knew, her life would never be the same.

"This cannot end well."

CHAPTER 22

To Liu's great surprise, the meeting *did* end well enough.

Though it got off to a questionable start. Mostly because Colton, in his yellow shirt, came through the door like a man auditioning for the lead role in a community production of *Flower Drum Song*, bowing to everything and everyone.

As the diminutive Chens looked on in surprise, the tall and gangly Colton greeted Kat and Paislee with an awkward bow. "Sisters," he said, as they watched with amusement.

He bowed slightly to Chun and Tao, putting his hand out to shake Tao's hand, and then quickly retracting it.

Colton bowed and nodded to Ling as Liu introduced them, welcoming Liu's mother to his ranch. His hands twitched as he started to touch Liu's arm for courage, then changed directions.

Liu tried not to smile as she searched the floor, trying to avoid eye contact with her family.

She wondered if he had regrets about barging in the way he did, with everyone staring. But then Liu felt a flash of anger at her family. They were behaving the way she'd expected, and so was he—but he was a good man. And if they at all made him feel unwelcome, she would be ashamed.

But as she opened her mouth to speak up on his behalf, someone beat her to it.

"*Ahh bah!*" Little Willow, who had been in Chun's arms, realized her favorite uncle was in the room and squealed in delight, while stretching her arms towards him.

"Well lookee here," Colton said to Willow, in equal delight.

Chun smiled at the baby's joy and handed her to Colton, who nodded in thanks, then walked with her into the living room. As he bounced her up and down in his arms, he seemed to forget all about his forced display, and merely talked to the baby. Setting her down again amidst her toys, he began playing with her—speaking in baby talk that she seemed to understand.

In moments, Chun, Tao, and Ling had joined the two on the floor and they were all playing together, tossing a ball for Willow to crawl after, and stacking blocks for her to knock down.

Liu exhaled with relief, until her mother came back in wearing a question on her face as she subtly gestured to Colton.

"*Zhè shì?*" Ling asked her nervous daughter—*what's going on here?*

Kat took in the scene and came to Colton and Liu's rescue.

"Colton," she exclaimed, "came to get Willow and me."

Looking at the mother and daughter, Kat continued. "Willow and I walked here earlier with the stroller, but now I don't have time to walk back. Colton came to bring us home to the ranch, didn't you Colton?"

"Uh, yeah, I did," Colton fumbled as he walked back into the kitchen. He'd really just wanted to be where the action was—he was a people person, after all, just as his mother had said. And with Ash in his summer business class, and Ridge off trying to purchase a little bungalow in town, all his *people* seemed to be at the cook house.

Pike lived at his new house now, with his bride, and was probably painting away in his art studio. And Gunnar was out in the basin, taking care of West Ranch business.

Colton had his builders and contractors working on the new development, but there just hadn't been anyone to talk to—until Liu came along. He had enjoyed dropping in on her, and being treated to small plates of her cooking. That is, until her family came to stay with her. Now she was nervous, like a long-tailed cat on a porch full of rocking chairs.

Ling looked skeptical, but nodded and went back to be with the baby. The three elder Chens were now getting Willow ready for her five-minute journey home.

"Hungry?" Liu whispered the question to him, out of earshot from her family.

"Always," Colton whispered back, which made her blush and smile. Somehow, she didn't think he was entirely talking about food. A few minutes later, as Liu walked with him to his truck, he said "I think they liked me."

"Everybody likes you, Colton," Liu said.

He nodded. Kat was still in the cook house, gathering Willow's things.

"I used to care about that sort of thing," he said, "but now I only care that *you* like me, Liu—and your family. They were very nice."

"Of course they were nice," she said with a note of sudden irritation in her voice, "you're the owner of the ranch. My employer."

Colton shook his head.

"Look," he said in exasperation. "This isn't corporate America, this is just a ranch full of hard-working people of equal importance, including yourself. If two of those people are attracted to each other, and want to go out for dinner..."

"...or kiss a little," Liu said with a small smile.

"Or kiss, *more* than just a little," Colton said, "then we should be able to explore whether or not it amounts to a hill of beans, or something more. I think you and I could be good together. You could be my good luck charm. I think you're my yellow shirt, Liu."

"I've never been called somebody's yellow shirt before," she teased.

"My point is this," Colton said, bringing an uncharacteristic tone of seriousness to their conversation. "Is it your family that objects to us, or is it you? Because I think you've been hiding behind them, Liu."

Liu stepped back and looked up at Colton, as though she'd been stung. But he went on.

"Maybe they are protective—most parents are," he said. "But you're a grown woman. I know because I've tasted your kisses, and trust me —they are the kisses of a woman, not a girl. And maybe they haven't always let you choose—most parents don't let their kids make important decisions until they're ready. But you're not a kid anymore. And I think you're ready, and they probably know you're ready, too. It's why they hold on so tight."

Liu was listening closely.

"My question to you is this," Colton said. "If they let you choose, would *you* choose me?"

CHAPTER 23

*L*iu thought he buried the lead.

The part of Colton's question that stood out wasn't the part about "would you choose me?" "*If they let you choose*" stood out like the proverbial sore thumb.

Liu had never pushed back against her parents' plans and dreams for her life. She'd even agreed to take a trip to China to meet a man there that her aunties had chosen for her.

"If you like, you bring him home," they said, making it clear that it was her decision. But Liu knew they expected her to bring him home unless there was a strong reason not to.

He seemed nice enough. Liu wrote to Bo a time or two, and he wrote back. She hoped his English was better spoken than written, and that was often the case. At the same time, he probably hoped she spoke more Chinese than she let on in her letters.

Bo was an accountant, like her mother. If he came to the states, he would be a guest of the Chens, and Ling would tutor him as he waited for citizenship, and earned the needed certifications to work in the U.S.

Then he and Liu would be a modern Chinese-American couple.

"Love would come," Ling assured her. "The aunties know."

But did they know? What if they were wrong?

How *could* they know? Liu wondered. The "aunties" had never met her. They only knew of her through conversations between her grandmother and distant relatives back in China—they didn't know Liu, or her hopes and dreams.

They didn't know how she wanted to have a successful business someday.

They didn't know that the music she liked was mostly American bands. Or that she thought it would be fun to add a pink streak to her jet-black hair before she turned 30. And maybe get a small diamond stud pierced on the top of her ear—if she could get the courage.

Not even her own parents knew all of her thoughts and dreams, so the Chinese aunties certainly could not. Therefore, they certainly didn't know a thing about her heart. She barely knew her own heart, she realized now.

The only thing she was sure of was the way her heart fluttered and leapt every time she saw Colton West.

CHAPTER 24

"So you're going to buy the Madison house?" Ash asked Ridge, as the two of them worked to pull up linoleum tiles in the little bungalow.

"I'm going to try," Ridge said. He was on his knees, and feeling the burn as he tugged, using muscles that hadn't done much more than get him in and out of his truck, or lift a burger, for months now. He knew he was going to pay for this tomorrow with a back ache and sore arms.

But working alongside Ash was worth a few twinges. Except for his grandmother, nobody had ever stuck by Ash. And Ridge was determined not to be a father in name only—he wanted the boy to know what it felt like to have somebody next to him.

Literally.

If he was successful in his bid to win the little house next door, he could keep a closer eye on Ash. After all, the boy still hadn't hit 18, and needed looking after. In the best possible world, the two could be future business partners. Build up a little something together.

The thought excited Ridge.

With the massive West holdings, his life had been about continuing the work already started for him. Ridge's own great grandfather,

Bluff Fletcher, laid the foundation and he carried on. Some, like Gunnar, found great satisfaction in carrying on the West legacy. Others, like Colton and Pike, wanted to break their own ground. Build their own domains.

As for Ridge, he'd never questioned the purpose of his life. He did as he was told and was taught. Maintain and expand West enterprises.

"Yes sir; yes maam," he had said.

Somehow the little Madison house signified a clean slate and a fresh start. Maybe even a little long overdue rebellion against a life he felt was carved in stone since the day he was born. He had thought it was too late to change directions, but then Ash came into his life, bringing all manner of possibilities.

He was no longer a husband, but he could still be a father. And with the little bungalow under his belt, suddenly he was a pioneer. Striking out on his own.

"Don't overdo it Dad," Ridge heard Ash say as he stopped tugging on the floor. "I don't want you to hurt yourself. And we both need a break."

Ridge sat back and leaned against the cupboards. He wiped his brow, and took a long drink of the water in his bottle nearby. Ash did the same. Looking around the little kitchen, Ridge caught a vision for Ash's master plan.

"They don't make cupboards like they used to," Ridge said. "These are beautifully crafted. They'll look great with a fresh coat of paint, and save you a ton of money."

Ash nodded. His plan was to replace the countertops and flooring, but save by refreshing the cabinets with paint and new hardware.

"I haven't figured out what to do about the walls yet," Ash said, looking around.

Ridge gazed up too. He suspected there was some nostalgia for the only home Ash ever knew growing up. The older man reminded himself that this house was home for Ash, and he shouldn't push him to go faster than he was comfortable with.

"Yep," Ridge said, gazing at the vintage wallpaper.

"I suppose if I wait long enough," Ash ventured, "roosters, grapes, and teapots will come back in style."

Ridge smiled at Ash. "You don't have to do this, you know, any of this," he said, gesturing to the room around them. "You can leave the house as is, and take your time. Make decisions when you're ready. I'd hate to see you change everything, then have regrets."

Ash smiled sadly.

"I appreciate that Dad," he said. "But I'm ready for this. So was Granny—these are all things she talked about doing someday anyway, before she lost track of things."

By "losing track of things," Ridge knew Ash was talking about the dementia his grandmother suffered from, and began exhibiting when Ash was an adolescent. The boy tried valiantly to care for her, until he got in over his head. That's when he ended up coming to the ranch with Gunnar.

"I'm just glad I get to keep the house," Ash said. "I didn't expect that. I thought for certain it would end up in the bank's hands."

Ridge smiled at Ash. He knew how much his grandmother loved and cared for him, so much that she put her estate in his name, to provide him with a future. If only she knew the wealth that would be at his fingertips one day as Ash West—she needn't have worried.

But the real inheritance she passed down was her love and devotion.

"Speaking of houses in the bank's hands," Ridge said with a mischievous grin, "I'd like to get a look inside that Madison house."

"But you said yourself nobody can see it before the auction," Ash responded.

"*Officially* that's true," Ridge said.

"Hmm," Ash said, "I don't know if I like the sound of that."

"I'm just suggesting a little sneak peek in the windows," Ridge said innocently, "now that it's dark out, I could saunter over with a ladder and a flashlight and catch a glimpse."

"Now I'm *certain* I don't like the sound of that," Ash said, feeling a paternal role reversal coming on.

In the not-so-distant past, Ash had his own casual relationship with right and wrong, and didn't always choose wisely. Peeking into the window of an abandoned house did not seem so heinous, but he didn't think it was a good look on the man he revered as his father.

Ridge West, town leader. Pillar of the community.

"Take it from me Dad," Ash said. "Choosing wrong over right is a slippery slope."

"Ash," Ridge assured the boy, "I'm going to buy the Madison house no matter what. I just want to see a little bit of what my money is buying. Whether it's a gut job, or a face lift."

"If you don't mind, I'm going to sit this dance out," Ash said as he put his work gloves back on and began pulling up floor tiles once again.

CHAPTER 25

*A*fter saying his goodbye's to Ash, Ridge made like he was heading to the ranch, but then parked his truck around the corner and got out again. He jogged quietly towards the backyard of the small Madison house.

Ridge took the light jacket that was in his hands and slipped it on. The night was clear, with a cool breeze pushing the air around. One of the benefits of living in the mountainous region was the temperate climate. Warm in the daytime, and cool sleeping weather at night.

When Randi was alive, the two would usually throw open their bedroom window before going to sleep, no matter how warm the day had been. This way they could hear the sounds of the rushing water in the gorge, as well as the Wyoming wildlife.

Owls hooted from the branches of pines.

Coyotes howled in the distance.

Cattle lowed from the open range where they grazed.

In the early autumn, they could hear the bugling of the bull elk as they gathered the females in their inner circle, and prepared for the competitive rutting season. This sound was one of Randi's particular favorites. For a few weeks in September, she and Ridge would head out after supper to find the herds. They'd set up their chairs and use binoculars to watch the ritual of the bugling from a safe distance.

"Look at that big fellow," Randi would point at a bull elk with his mighty antlers. "He's gathering the girls."

Ridge would just enjoy the wonder of seeing these animals from her perspective. Back in northern Michigan, Randi had seen deer and a bear or two, but never the great herds of magnificent creatures that migrated through Wyoming every year.

Not so long ago, these memories of his beloved wife, gone five years now, would reduce him to tears and depression for days. But as they say, time heals all wounds. And while he'd never feel completely healed from the great loss of his sweetheart, he was at the point where he could look back at their happy days with gratitude.

And without feeling utterly devastated.

The Madison house was dark. There was no light coming through the closed drapes.

Seeing that there wasn't a soul in sight, only gentle sounds coming through the open windows of neighboring houses, Ridge exhaled his nervousness and stood up straighter. With the drapes shut tight, he could only get a look at the exterior, he supposed.

"I'm not doing anything wrong," he said quietly to himself, "just taking a look at my next investment."

Under cover of darkness.

Walking around to the back window, adrenaline shot through Ridge and he froze. The curtains were parted slightly, meaning he could get a look into what would surely be the kitchen—the costliest room to renovate. But it was too high up to see in.

Eyeing the situation, Ridge recalled seeing a wooden ladder earlier when it was still light out. It was leaning against the outside shed at Ash's bungalow. He could sneak over and retrieve the ladder—surely Ash wouldn't mind—and tiptoe back through the tall grass to the Madison house. In the dark, as it was, nobody would see him climb up and shine a light into the house.

"One quick peek, and then home," he said to himself.

He turned to go back to Ash's shed.

A dog barked from the yard of a nearby home, and Ridge jumped.

Stopping to take a deep breath, he told himself how silly he was being. "There's no call to be nervous," he said to himself. He'd take a quick gander at the abandoned home, and he'd have more of an idea of how to move forward at midnight, when the online bidding started.

"I'm just looking at my own house," he said to himself, reaching the ladder. "In a few short hours, I'll have placed the highest bid and the house will be mine—free and clear."

Extricating the ladder from Ash's shed wasn't a slam-dunk, Ridge quickly realized, causing his anxiety to rise again. The ladder hadn't moved in a few years and the lower rung was embedded in weeds.

Dang, Ridge said under his breath. He was considering abandoning his undercover maneuver, when the ladder finally released itself from the grass. Ridge nearly tumbled backwards into Ash's lawn, but caught himself in time. Though not without coming down hard on his already sore knee.

"Ooh," he said under his breath, "that's going to hurt tomorrow."

Limping slightly, Ridge tucked the ladder under one arm and made his way back to the Madison house. When did wooden ladders become so heavy? He wondered to himself. There was a time when he could lift all manner of heavy things on the ranch with ease. And even grace. Something he was without tonight.

Reaching the house, Ridge looked around once again to make sure he was alone. The barking dog had gone back inside for the night. A few of the houses had turned off their porch lights, and some were dark altogether. He could see television screens broadcasting the late-night news through gauzy curtains.

But nobody paid any mind to Ridge West and his ladder, as he leaned it against the back wall of the house.

Feeling in his pocket for the small flashlight he had the foresight to bring, Ridge settled the ladder into sturdy ground, and stepped on the first rung. His leg muscles and sore knee protested, but he only had to go up a few rungs to be able to peek in.

On the second rung, the ladder shifted in the earth and Ridge panicked slightly. The movement stopped though, and he went up one more rung. He was face to face with the kitchen curtains, and moments away from getting the glance he'd been waiting to see.

Flashlight in hand, though turned off, something caught his eye—it was a flash of diffused light coming from inside the house.

Could that be right—were his eyes playing tricks on him?

Ridge's heart was beating fast, and he struggled to control his breathing. But there—he saw the light again! Somebody was definitely inside the Madison house. The intruder was wearing all black, and had a flashlight in his hands.

Someone had broken in, he realized with alarm. Should he call the police?

Just as he wondered this, the flashlight turned towards him—illuminating him. The light blinded Ridge and revealed his presence at the window.

The intruder inside the house screamed, startling him off his perch.

He heard a second scream that sounded like a little girl.

Just as he realized that the high-pitched scream was his own, he hit the ground.

CHAPTER 26

"*R*owdy, Gray! How long has it been?" Gunnar clapped his cousins on the back.

"Years, Gunnar." Brothers Rowdy and Gray West tripped over each other's words along with Gunnar as they reunited. Rowdy didn't want to mention that the last time they saw each other was as Randi's funeral, so he left it alone.

Gunnar introduced Kat to the men, and she in turn introduced them to little Willow, who was on her way to bed.

"Ah, sorry for arriving so late at night," Gray said to Kat. "What terrible manners we have. Only, we had to wait for the weather in Montana to clear for takeoff."

Pilot Gray West had flown he and Rowdy to West Ranch in his Cessna TTx.

"Not at all," Kat said. "I am so pleased to meet you at last. Gunnar has spoken about you so often. And Ridge will be delighted to have you at his party tomorrow."

"Dad meant to be here to welcome you," Gunnar said with a shrug. "I don't know where he is. He's been talking about seeing you for weeks."

Just then, Colton and Pike walked in with loud and boisterous greetings.

"Well look what the wind blew in," Colton said to his cousins, to more hugs and back slapping.

"Where's Dad and Ash?" Pike wanted to know, but Gunnar could only shrug.

"Dad's not answering his phone," he told his brother. "I guess he'll be home late."

The five West men who were in the room filled up the space with laughter as they talked over one another.

At nearly 40, Rowdy West was officially retiring from the roping and rodeo circuit. He'd made a small fortune to add to the larger fortune their family in Montana held—especially since selling off the majority of the Montana land in recent years.

"We kept enough acreage for the home, and for recreation," Gray chimed in, "but as far as being a working ranch, those days are gone." All the men gave a moment of silence to respect the passing of the formerly lucrative West Ranch of Montana, but there was too much to talk about to remain silent for long.

"I can't do the rodeo traveling like I used to," Rowdy told his cousins good-naturedly. "So I'll stay put. I just don't know where it is that I'll be *staying put*, but I'll figure that out."

Gunnar noticed Rowdy had a slight limp.

"Gray," Colton said, "I can't wait to kick the tires on that airplane tomorrow. That's one sweet ride."

Gray grinned wide. He was as proud of his Cessna as Gunnar was of Willow.

"I'll take you up in it, Colton," Gray said. "Give you a birds-eye-view of this ranch of yours."

Slightly older than Gunnar and younger than Rowdy, Gray was the more easy-going of the brothers. Until, that is, he was up in an airplane fighting the autumn wildfires that frequented the west. Which was dangerous and serious business.

"I'm just glad Gray didn't land us in the gorge," Rowdy said to laughter.

"I'm just glad one of your ranch hands came along with his Jeep, and gave us a ride to the house from the basin," Gray said, to more laughter. "It was looking like a long, dusty walk."

FROM HER BEDROOM, Kat settled into her bed with a good book. It was earlier than she usually turned in, but getting ready for Ridge's birthday party these past weeks had kept her hopping.

The weather report looked clear for the big event, Liu and her family had been cooking for days, and the long-lost Montana cousins had arrived to make the family party complete. If only someone knew where the birthday boy himself was. He disappeared in the afternoon to help Ash at the bungalow, but said he'd be home much earlier.

Ridge would not be happy to think they were worried about him, or fussing over his absence. "I'm a grown man," she could practically hear him protesting. And he'd be right. He was with Ash—so she could sleep knowing he was okay.

A burst of laughter from the kitchen reminded her that Gunnar would not be joining her anytime soon. The cousins were enjoying a long-overdue gathering, that sounded like good medicine for all the men involved.

Kat was glad.

Gunnar and Pike had grown very close in the past months since Pike's marriage, even though he left the everyday operations of the ranch solely on Gunnar's shoulders. She knew that her husband missed Colton too, but the younger brother was so happy now that he was making his own way, and developing West Gorge Woods.

Their new endeavors had left a void, but also gone was the tension Gunnar sometimes felt at his brothers' tepid love for the daily workload.

"Better to hire it out," Kat had said, which proved easier said than done.

Another burst of laughter showed no waning in the conversation or enthusiasm, so Kat rolled over and turned her light off. She left a small light burning on Gunnar's side of the bed, for when he came in.

CHAPTER 27

With a little snort, Ridge West jerked awake. Immediately, his hand flew to his neck to massage a kink in his aching muscles.

He could see daylight through the window of the holding room, but his situation hadn't improved much since the night before. He was still in the West Gorge jail, dozing while sitting upright on a hard bench. It had been years since he'd slept sitting straight up, most likely on a horse during the busy season. He hadn't missed it at all.

Next to him, the woman in a black hooded sweatshirt also stirred.

They both turned to look as they heard steps coming down the cement-floored hallway.

"Wakee wakee," officer Jason Scott said as he walked. He carried a tray in one hand with two cups of coffee and two muffins, which he slipped through the opening between the bars. The woman slowly got up and took the tray, thanking the officer. She offered a coffee to Ridge, who accepted with a begrudging grunt of thanks.

Jason shook his head at the pair, and broke into a grin.

"Well what d'ya know," the officer said. "I've got West Gorge royalty in my humble little jail. Ridge West, the founder of the town, and Casey Parks, leading town realtor."

"Look, officer..." Ridge started to say, "has anybody called about getting me out?"

"No, Mr. West," Jason said. "I'd say you chose your one phone call very badly. Same as you, Miss Parks."

"Thank you, officer," the woman said smoothly, "I'll just wait until you drop the charges."

"There are no charges against you, yet..." the officer said, "but I can't let you two out until we go through the proper channels. Breaking and Entering is a serious offense, miss. And Mr. West, we don't cotton to *peeping Toms* in this town."

"But I didn't..." Casey Parks began to protest, but was cut off.

"But I wasn't..." Ridge said at the same time, stepping on her words.

"Save it for the judge," Officer Scott said, and then went to answer his ringing phone.

Left alone, Ridge and Casey sat side by side and sipped their coffees. The two had barely acknowledged the other in the commotion of the night before—not while sitting together in the squad car, or having their phones taken away.

Why Gunnar hadn't picked up the phone, Ridge didn't know. He should have called Kat, now that he thought of it. Or Ash. He half expected Ash to come outside during the scuttle, as both he and the woman were squished into the squad car. The boy must have been wearing his headphones.

It was so humiliating, Ridge thought. Thank goodness it had been dark outside.

Venturing a glance, he looked over at Casey Parks who was glancing back at him.

"Maam," Ridge nodded and went back to his coffee. She was rather pretty. Perhaps around 50 years old, give or take. She had enough lines on her face to make her interesting, and piercing eyes that seemed to see the humor in life. If Ridge didn't dislike her as he did, he might have offered her a weak smile.

"So," she said in a gravelly voice, sounding like someone who had spent the night sitting up on a bench, "you're the great town founder

I've heard so much about. I always thought we'd meet at a rotary luncheon, or city council meeting. Not an abandoned house. And not in jail."

"And you're the realtor buying up all the affordable housing in town to create vacation rentals, leaving our hard-working citizens homeless," Ridge answered with an edge in his voice.

"Really Mr. West," she said. "I have six little houses—hardly a monopoly. I wish I could buy others, but I can't afford them."

"You were trying to buy the Madison house, though," Ridge said.

"Only at a good price," she said. "If the floors need leveling, that would eat up too much of my renovation budget."

"Is that why you broke in?" Ridge asked.

"I didn't *technically* break in—the door was unlocked." Casey sounded agitated. "I just took a quick walk-through before the bidding started, until I was frightened by your face."

Ridge chuckled.

"Well, maybe I'm not as handsome as I used to be, but I've never had a woman scream before when she got a look at me," he said.

"Any woman would scream, seeing a man's face peering through an eight-foot-tall window, in the dark!"

"I reckon," Ridge said. "And any man would fall off a ladder, hearing a woman scream like you did."

"I suppose," Casey said. And then, after a few minutes, "Are you okay?"

"No," Ridge said, "I hurt all over, thanks to that fall."

The two were silent then, thinking about the events of the night before, and how they'd gotten into the mess they were in. Ridge was lucky to have only bruises and aches from his tumble, instead of breaks and cuts.

Casey mentioned the bidding, which was going on without him.

"Say," Casey asked, "why do you want that little house anyway? You own so much already. Plus a sprawling, beautiful home on your ranch, or so I hear. I've never seen it myself."

"For a hobby. I wanted a shared interest with my youngest son, so we could spend time before he graduates high school," Ridge said.

Casey nodded thoughtfully for a minute.

"Have you considered taking up fishing?"

Ridge laughed a little, in spite of his resolve to hate Casey Parks.

"Well, Ash doesn't want to go fishing. He wants to build a business. He wants to channel his pain and fears into something productive. And I want to help him… work alongside him, like I did with my own dad."

Casey listened quietly.

"Ash is my youngest," Ridge clarified, though why he felt the need to tell her so much, he didn't know. "He inherited the bungalow next door to the Madison house. He's going to renovate it and turn it into a rental—like yours. I just wanted to have a project of my own nearby, to keep an eye on him."

"Hmm," Casey nodded.

"But I suppose neither of us are buying that house," Ridge said, "seeing as how you and I were stuck behind bars while the bidding took place."

"Right," Casey said, but looked uncomfortable.

Just then, Officer Scott came walking down the hallway. "Gunnar West is here to pick you up Mr. West. You're free to go."

Ridge sat up straighter and smiled, trying his best to offer an olive branch to Casey. "Someone must be coming for you soon, I hope. You did call someone, right?"

"I did," Casey said. "I called my assistant… to bid on the Madison house in my absence."

Ridge's mouth fell open as he realized she'd gotten the better of him, and bought the house he wanted so desperately.

"Well!" Ridge said through gritted teeth. "Happy birthday to me."

CHAPTER 28

G unnar drove through the town of West Gorge with Ridge in the front seat of the truck, who was glowering and gazing out the side window.

"Stop at the drugstore, will you?" The father grumbled.

"Sure thing," Gunnar answered, bemused. He never in a million years thought he'd have to get his father out of jail, for invading private property and peeping into windows, of all things. Ridge had been unusually silent since leaving the police station, and Gunnar was reluctant to break the ice. Though he had a million questions.

He was feeling a bit groggy himself, having been awaken earlier than expected. After a late night of catching up with his Montana cousins, Gunnar had hoped for a few more hours of sleep. Apparently, however, Ridge had called him late the night before but Gunnar had not heard his phone while laughing with his boisterous brothers and cousins.

Ridge hopped out of the tall truck and groaned, then started to limp towards the pharmacy. Gunnar thought he'd better follow and keep an eye on him. Once in the store, Gunnar waved at the owner and pharmacist while Ridge went to find aspirin and a bottle of water.

"Hey Bud," Gunnar said, and Bud nodded and smiled.

Bud Shire had come dangerously close to being Gunnar's father-in-law, and the older man would have been the only good thing to come out of that alliance.

After dating Bud's daughter Darlene for a year or so, Gunnar had been about to pop the question. He really did think that while Darlene wasn't perfect, she might be as good as it gets in the small town. And Gunnar was lonely.

Luckily for him, Darlene rejected the idea, and took off for a job in the big city.

By the time Darlene returned with her tail between her legs, ready to concede and settle down at the West Ranch, Gunnar had met the beautiful doctor Kat Tate—and meeting Kat changed the course of his life forever.

Now, he is amazed every day at his good fortune that the woman he fell head over heels in love with, actually loves him back. Every day and every night. When she slips into his arms, he can't believe his dumb luck—that a cowboy such as himself could earn the adoration of such a beautiful and accomplished woman.

And better still, she was now the mother of his lovely daughter, Willow West.

Bud Shire was a good man, but seeing him in the drugstore was a reminder to Gunnar of how close he had come to making the biggest mistake of his life. Darlene Shire would always be a cautionary tale—the "dodged bullet" he thanks God that he missed.

Back in the truck with Ridge, who was opening a bottle of aspirin, Gunnar drove for a few miles and then couldn't take it any longer.

"Hey… happy birthday, Dad," he ventured.

"Hmm," Ridge grunted. And then, "thanks, son. And thank you for coming to get me from the… the…"

"*Jail?*" Gunnar volunteered, trying to keep the smile out of his voice.

"Bah!" Ridge grumbled again. "Jail. Me in jail. Can you imagine Gunnar?"

"No sir," Gunnar said. "That's a bet I would have lost."

Ridge chuckled at that, in spite of his frustration. "Me too."

"Well, I have to say I'm mighty curious," Gunnar continued. "But you don't have to tell me anything if you don't want to. I imagine you might only want to tell the story once, if at all. You'll have a crowd of itching ears at your party later."

Ridge nodded. "Let's just say I'm an old fool, who should have listened to the wisdom of his youngest son, and leave it at that."

"Fair enough," Gunnar said, relieved that Ash had stayed out of it.

Whatever *it* was.

CHAPTER 29

"*Happy birthday to you,*
    Happy birthday to you,
  Happy birthday dear Ridge, happy birthday to you!"

THE COLLECTION of Wests from near and far, along with twenty or so guests from West Gorge, all raised their glasses to toast the patriarch. Over the course of the evening, the guest of honor seemed to have loosened up and was enjoying himself immensely.

In spite of his night in the slammer.

To his credit, officer Jason Scott, who had been an invited guest along with his parents, Marta and Nels, apparently hadn't said a word to his busy-body mother about having to cuff the birthday boy the night before, and tuck him in the back of his cruiser.

"Happy birthday Mr. West," the officer said simply, then went to find more dumplings.

"Thank you, Jason," Ridge had replied, secretly glad that Marta hadn't asked him if he needed to be added to the town prayer chain. Landing on the West Gorge prayer chain, Ridge knew, was like wearing gloves made of sticky fly paper—it was hard to shake. Though she did give him a fright when she arrived.

"Ridge West, I heard a rumor about you," Marta said loudly when she got there, causing Ridge to jump a mile. He braced himself for the worst. "I heard a rumor it was your *birthday!*" She came over and gave him a hug, while Nels shook his hand.

Ridge exhaled with relief.

"Guilty," he said, regretting his choice of words.

It was Paislee who saved him. Blithely waltzing over, she took his arm and lead him to the dance floor. It was a beautiful summer night, and the sun was starting to set behind the mountains. Ridge looked up to see the lights shining through the paper lanterns and smiled.

"Should we get this party started?" She asked with a smile.

"With pleasure," he answered. Over the course of the past months, Ridge had grown very fond of his newest daughter-in-law. At first, he was afraid that the society girl, the heiress, would look down her nose at their more down-home rustic ways. But Paislee West quickly became one of the family.

A morning person like himself, Paislee was almost always in the kitchen when he woke up at the crack of dawn, making coffee and popping biscuits in the oven.

"I got pretty good at biscuits while living in the West barn this past winter," she told him, recalling her snowed-in honeymoon with Pike. "I burnt a batch or two in that old woodstove," she laughed, "but I caught on."

When the snow had melted, she and Pike showed up at West Ranch, and lived at the family home while drawing up plans for their modern farmhouse and art studio. That's when Ridge and the Wests really got to know Paislee, and fall in love with her just as Pike had.

For several months, first light was their time—just Ridge and Paislee, and fresh cups of coffee. One after the other.

She enjoyed waiting on him, and wouldn't let him do anything for himself.

"No no no, you sit down," she'd insist, bringing him a mug, along with cream and sugar. "I just love early mornings here in Wyoming, don't you Ridge?"

Her enthusiasm for life was contagious. She wanted to know every bit of West family history, and all about the surrounding land. Paislee also asked Ridge to tell her stories about Randi. And the questions she asked were unusual, loosening an avalanche of long forgotten memories.

"What was she wearing when you first saw her? What was her favorite song? What horse did she ride on the ranch?" Paislee's questions were endless—that is, until she detected a sadness in Ridge at the loss he felt. Then she would change the subject, while still retaining her beautiful smile.

Ridge missed Paislee more than he thought he would when she and Pike moved out of the ranch and into their new home. He told her this as they danced together. For once, Paislee was speechless, and he could swear she had a tear in her eye.

"I'm glad I didn't wear out my welcome," she said quietly.

"Never," Ridge said. "You are family, and you've made Pike a very happy man. I didn't know he had *happiness* in him, truth be told. I've been worried about him for a very long time, you know."

They were quiet for a few minutes as they contemplated Ridge's statement.

"I'll bet you have some happiness left in you, Ridge," Paislee said at last.

"Oh, I'm too old for happiness," he replied. "I'll settle for a dance with a pretty girl every now and again, and the occasional piece of chocolate cake."

"In that case," Paislee said, "let's dance on over and get a piece before it's gone."

Ridge laughed, but let her take the lead.

On the far side of the pavilion, Liu, along with her mother and grandmother, were running a tight ship. They kept the Chinese pork skewers hot and slathered in BBQ sauce, while keeping the noodle salads cold and crisp. Liu's dumplings were tender and tasty, and going like hotcakes.

The guests were devouring the spring rolls, the sticky rice, and the cucumber salad too. But it was the chocolate cake that had Liu on pins and needles.

She had longed to modify Cindy's recipe, and even tried a few versions with less sugar, and flour substitutes. "Still too sweet," her family would say. But it was Ridge West who would make the final declaration. And his word would determine whether Liu had been a success or not at her first West family function.

"Well, it just looks beautiful, Liu," Ridge said as the chef handed him a slice.

He could have sworn Liu's hands were trembling, which surprised him.

As he lifted the fork, he looked over to see that the normally busy Chen family had frozen in their tracks, and were watching him take his first bite. He didn't want to eat in front of an audience, but he was in too deep.

"Okay," he said to himself, "here goes nothing."

With fear and trepidation, Ridge put a large bite of cake into his mouth and prepared for the worst. He had heard stories of what the Chens considered to be *cake*, and just didn't think he could stomach arrowroot flour and beet juice on his birthday.

He chewed, and chewed some more.

Was he imagining things?

No, he decided. It was wonderful. Even better than Cindy's cake, if that was possible. Slowly, Ridge began nodding as he chewed. He smiled as he speared another bite with his fork. "Mmmm," he managed to mumble appreciatively.

Looking up, he saw that Liu's grandmother and mother were spellbound, holding onto each other as if the fate of the world depended on his reaction. And he knew then how much expectation to succeed sat on Liu's shoulders.

This wasn't just a cake he was eating; it was Liu's career validation. It was her self-worth. Her final exam—pass or fail. It would determine whether the Chens accepted Liu's independence, and whether or not Liu herself felt proud of the job she was doing.

The piece of cake in his hands was a ticking explosive, and he was the bomb squad.

Knowing every one of his movements was being tracked, Ridge ate every single bite of the cake, and then used the tines of the fork to skate over the surface, picking up all the crumbs. Then, and only then, did Ridge turn to Liu, with the plate in his open hands. Bowing slightly to honor the chef, he politely asked for another piece.

As she served him, Ridge could detect a smile in the young cook's eyes, and a tear trickling down the cheek of her mother.

"Excellent cake," he declared, "a triumph."

CHAPTER 30

*L*iu stood in the background of the party for most of the evening with her mother and grandmother. The young chef commanded a team of Ash's friends and hired assistants like General Patton.

She was all business until eventually, as with all parties, many of the guests began to wander towards their cars, and helpers were sent home. The food was cleared and stored in coolers. The cake was decimated, Colton was pleased to see, but for a few pieces that Liu had packaged up to put in the ranch house refrigerator.

And as the night wound down, the few who remained were mostly family and the small band. The party was drawing to a close, Colton knew, and there would only be a few dances left, and Chens or no Chens, he longed to share a dance with Liu.

"No, Colton," she had said as nicely as she could earlier in the evening, "I am working."

Then again later, she shook her head at his unasked question.

But near the end, he could tell that her resolve was weakening. Her smile was bigger and more relaxed—especially after receiving praise from Ridge about her cake.

A triumph, his dad said.

And without an army to lead, or food to serve, Colton pointed out that her lovely, graceful hands were empty.

"*Please* dance with me Liu," he said again, reaching for her with his arms and pleading with his eyes. And then, like a miracle, she gave in to him.

Barely acknowledging the disapproval of her mother and grand-mother, Liu threw off her apron like a shackle that had been tethering her to the ground, and flew into his arms with the most radiant grin he'd yet to see from her.

Liu's petite arms did their best to encircle his broad shoulders. His arms had no trouble wrapping around her tiny waist and pulling her close. Liu's feet were light and delicate as he moved her this way and that on the parquet flooring. Colton was mindful not to step on her polished toes, which were like beautiful incandescent pearls.

Was it just him, he wondered, or did the rest of the world fall away as they swayed and laughed together? If he was a betting man, he'd swear she'd say the same thing.

While holding Liu in his arms, Colton refrained from kissing the cook, and nuzzling his bleach blonde whiskers against her smooth golden skin. But he smiled with abandon, and allowed his eyes to drink her in—memorizing every raven-black lock of her hair that flew up as he twirled her around and around.

CHAPTER 31

*T*he sun shone brightly on the quiet Wyoming highway the morning after Ridge West's birthday celebration.

Ling Chen drove with Zhang's parents, Chun and Tao, in the backseat. They both had fallen asleep as soon as Ling got off the gravel road and onto the smooth straightaway.

"Just like toddlers," Ling thought with a smile, looking in the rearview mirror. The two were still so robust, always moving and contributing. But they were getting older, and tired easily. In a few hours, Chun and Tao would be back home in Rock Springs, and could rest some more.

Ling thought about a phrase the Americans used: the *sandwich generation*, where a person was stuck between their children and parents, and their needs. She was the baloney, and they were the bread.

Smiling at the word picture, Ling thought how Americans rarely understood that the Chinese in their midst were always in the middle. The time to shine, as it were, was in the afterlife. Because until then, they were always appeasing another generation. That's just how it was.

But the Chen family had been delighted to help Liu with her event.

It gave them a chance to see where she was living, and meet the family she was spending time with.

It had been an honor to help Liu, and they all hated to leave.

Maybe Liu was not so sad.

"Young people," Chun had told Ling before she'd fallen asleep, "want to be on their own. They think it's a sign of achievement. In my day," the elder had said, "it was a sign of failure to be alone."

Chun had said this in Chinese.

"Yes, Mama," Ling had responded.

Chun, in her day, wouldn't dream of becoming a leftover unmarried girl, and had therefore eagerly agreed to an arrangement with Tao. The two seemed very compatible to Ling, but then, she was their daughter-in-law. She hadn't known them when they were a young married couple, learning to meld their lives.

When it came to be Ling's turn to marry, her own parents were amenable to a match with Zhang Chen. This was convenient, because the two had been attracted to each other after becoming friends during their time at university.

Their wedding day was joyous, and filled with red flowers, lucky red money packets, and firecrackers in the street.

Ling began the day wearing a red silk kimono. As money packets were being offered to her, she sat alone on a wedding bed which had been jumped upon earlier by babies and toddlers of family and friends, for good luck and fertility—both of which they'd been blessed with.

Later in the day, in a white gown, there was a banquet in a hall decorated with red ribbons, gold paper lanterns, and electric candles. It was a wedding day Ling would never forget.

Like any mother, Ling was anxious for her daughter to know such happiness. And to know it while Chun and Tao were still living, so that they could be at peace in their next life. But because Liu had a strong affinity for the American culture, Ling and Zhang allowed Liu the freedom to form a love match with a boy in their community.

When that didn't occur, they allowed her another chance to find a husband during her college years, and then again at the culinary institute.

But still, Liu remained unmarried, and the grandparents had growing concerns. At last, Chun reached out to matchmaker Auntie Jun in China, who wanted Liu to fly there and meet Bo.

Bo was an accountant, like Ling herself. He had a respectable family, but longed to live in the United States. He had heard much about America, and Wyoming. He had distant cousins who lived in Rock Springs, who would house him until his wedding to Liu could be planned.

And while Liu had not made any promises, she had been dutiful and written back and forth letters with Bo, breaking the ice.

But Ling could now see trouble brewing in the form of Colton West.

Colton had brazenly come to meet Liu's family while they stayed at the cook house. Ling thought it very forward to come without being invited. She could hardly object; it was a house belonging to the West family, after all. And the Wests were Liu's employers.

As Colton spoke with Liu and Ling, as well as with Chun and Tao, Ling watched him carefully. There did not seem to be any untoward behavior on his part, which gave her relief. And Liu seemed to have the upper hand in their conversations, which also relieved her—Ling was happy to see that her daughter did not seem uncomfortable or intimidated around Colton.

Just the opposite, in fact, which also made Ling wary.

Liu's eyes and demeanor lit up in the cowboy's presence, much like her own demeanor had come alive when she was being courted by Zhang many years ago. And still today. But this would not do. Surely Liu must know the expectations they all had for her, to marry within their own community.

She would have to speak with Zhang when she returned home. He wasn't due back from California for several weeks, so she would call him and explain her fears for their daughter. Liu's father seemed to be able to reason with the girl better than anyone.

Ling would try to tell Zhang about the look in Colton's eyes at the birthday party, as he gazed from the background at Liu's every move —how he grinned with delight at the praise Ridge bestowed on their daughter over her *triumphant* cake, and gave her a "thumbs up" gesture.

How, after many of the guests had gone, Colton came to ask Liu to dance with him. Ling was sure Liu would refuse—she was working after all!

But his gesture was sweet and insistent, Ling had to admit, as he held his open hands and bowed to her. At last, Liu removed her apron, and fell into his arms as they waltzed and twirled to a song Ling didn't know.

She would tell her husband how the look in their eyes reminded her so much of the loving way Zang looked at her, and that was why they had to take the situation very seriously. And encourage Liu to fly to China soon to meet and bring back Bo, so their family could be happy.

But would Liu be happy?

Ling shook her head and pushed back the nagging thought. It was far too late for that to be a concern.

CHAPTER 32

"*N*ow it's my turn to ask a favor of you," Colton said to Liu the day after the party, while standing on her doorstep. Liu was drying her hands on a towel, eyeing Colton somewhat warily, he thought, even though her family had already left for Rock Springs and she was alone.

"Come in," she said, backing away from the door and then walking towards the kitchen.

Colton remained near the doorway as Liu tidied up her food preparations.

"Hungry?" She asked him.

"I'll grab something later," he smiled and said, which surprised Liu. "I need an expert opinion, and came to kidnap you for an hour, if you can spare it. You don't need to change," Colton said, "we'll just be on West land."

Liu raised her eyebrows in curiosity, and then smiled. Her heart had sped up at the sound of Colton's truck pulling up to the cook house, and then again as she watched him getting out of the truck and heading towards her.

Her smile broadened even more to see him in a yellow West Development Co. shirt—she knew it was his work uniform, but she had a hunch he was afraid to wear any other color but yellow since he met her family. It was so much in Colton's nature to want to be liked, and to please others. And she'd never been the object of anyone's desire to please.

Liu was exhausted from the party preparations, and her family's visit—and going for a drive sounded like just the break she needed.

Minutes later, they were driving together in Colton's truck. They both gazed at the changing landscape as the truck traveled from the cook house, past the guest house and the main house, and then beyond any outbuildings.

Looking around, Liu could spot grazing cattle far on the horizon.

The road became rockier and Colton slowed down for the last few miles before stopping. The mountains were close, and they could both hear the running water of the gorge.

"This is still West land?" Liu asked, incredulous at their vast holdings.

"Yep," Colton answered, "as far as the eye can see.

At last, Colton stopped his truck at a breathtaking vantage point on West property and they got out together. Ahead of her, the mountains and the gorge stood out in all their splendor.

To get to where they were, Colton had driven along the paved ranch road for several miles. Then they branched off onto a gravel road that seemed groomed and well-traveled. The next and final turn was a two-track road that led them to this spot.

"Well," Colton said, looking at Liu. "What do you think?"

"I think we're in the middle of nowhere," she said. "I'd say we're lost, but I see a picnic table and stakes in the ground—so, someone's been here before us."

"Come over to the table," Colton said, "I've got something to show you."

Once there, Colton unrolled a scroll of blueprints.

"I'm building my house right here," he said, gesturing to the stakes in the ground. "It seems secluded, but this site is situated between the ranch house and the town of West Gorge."

"What a beautiful spot," Liu said. She walked away from the table and took in the view once again. "It's magnificent Colton."

Colton watched her face as she spoke. Liu's at-times icy demeanor seemed to melt at the view of the gorge, with the water flowing over the rocks and through the crevices. A summer breeze picked up a few strands of her midnight hair, and she pushed them out of her eyes.

Liu seemed mesmerized.

"I was hoping you'd like it... I mean, I wanted to show you my kitchen, and get your advice," Colton said carefully, "as a professional, that is."

What he wanted to say was, "someday I'll ask you to share my home," but it was too soon for that.

"I can only hope the kitchen windows face this view," Liu said, turning to face Colton. "It's even more breathtaking than the spot where we had our picnic."

She blushed as she said this, perhaps remembering the sweetness of their first kiss.

He smiled his response.

"Let me walk you through my plans," he said, taking her hand. "Now over here, I have a wall of windows facing the gorge. The windows sit over the sink, then a coffee bar, and a six-burner cook top—is that big enough? Another wall of windows is an accordion door-wall that opens onto an outdoor kitchen."

"An *outdoor* kitchen too?" Liu gasped in surprise. "With a brick pizza oven?"

"Great idea," Colton said, writing a note on his plans. "Brick... oven."

"What's over here?" Liu walked to another stake in the ground.

"That is a butler's pantry," Colton said, "with storage enough for every small appliance known to man, and a separate..."

"...workstation?" she asked, hopefully.

"Yes. A separate workstation, away from the main room," he said, getting caught up in her excitement.

"Tell me about the island," Liu said to Colton, sounding giddy.

"You tell me, Liu," he coaxed her gently. "What should it be?"

"A *massive* quartz surface," Liu said with a smile, "with an overhang for half a dozen stools—a place for kids to do homework, and have their after-school snacks."

"Their dumplings, maybe?" He asked.

Liu caught herself just then. She was getting carried away, and that was unlike her. She cleared her throat to regain her composure, but Colton just smiled. He'd gotten what he wanted.

"What else does *your* house have?" Liu asked with great control.

"Right now, you're standing in the large family room," Colton said.

"With my shoes on," she said with a small smile and a *tsk tsk*.

"We can let it slide this one time," he said. "Over here is a home office, with room for a double desk and a million books."

Liu nodded with approval.

"And if you'll come this way," Colton said, offering Liu his arm and leading her across the dirt and sage brush growth, "you'll see the master bedroom—it also has a view of the mountains."

"This is a very grand house," Liu said.

"Yep," Colton agreed. "But I plan on staying here always, and raising my family. I want everyone to have what they need, and room to grow."

Liu suddenly seemed uncomfortable standing in Colton's bedroom, although it was just a patch of sagebrush with wooden stakes in the corners. She let go of his arm and walked back to the kitchen.

"Did I forget anything?" He asked her quietly.

"You've thought of everything," she answered.

And everyone, Colton thought to himself with a sly smile.

CHAPTER 33

$\mathcal{T}$he day after the birthday party, the ranch fridge was filled with boxed lunches from Liu, who knew the cowboys would be scattering to the far winds that day.

Ash had left first thing in the morning for the bungalow. He was a little bleary-eyed from keeping late hours with his brothers and cousins, but rising early was getting in his blood.

"It's the West curse," Gunnar told him with a laugh and clap on the back the night before when the subject came up. "If you're gonna to soar with the eagles..." Gunnar yelled to the crowd—by this time, mostly family, "...you still gotta *rise* with the *roosters!*" all the West men yelled back in unison, then laughed together.

Colton and Gray were also up early. The two were making their way to the Cessna for a flight, as promised by the older cousin. After they landed again, Gray wanted Colton to show him the town of West Gorge, and the housing development Colton was heading up.

Pike and Paislee told the two to be sure and stop by the farmhouse for a tour and a bite to eat. They wanted see the latest work in Pike's studio.

"I'm glad your cousins came," Kat said to Gunnar as they reluctantly climbed out of bed the morning after the party. "I like having them here."

"Me too," Gunnar said. "I'm glad they're not rushing off. I'd like for Rowdy to spend some time with me on the ranch. He misses the day-to-day operations of the Montana ranch and I can sure keep him busy while he's here."

"Don't work him to death, Gunnar," Kat said with a laugh. "This is his vacation."

Gunnar laughed.

"The West men don't take vacations," he said. "You ought to know that."

Kat nodded.

"About that…"

"Yes, about that," Gunnar said. "Just as soon as I can find someone to help me run the place, you and I and Willow are going to take a trip. Wherever you want to go."

Soon after, Gunnar and Rowdy were heading out on horseback to see more of the ranch. They planned on coming back after a short ride to transfer to one of the Jeeps—Rowdy had taken a spill or two in his time on the rodeo circuit, and could only ride for a few hours without aches and pains shooting up his legs and spine.

"Can you imagine, Gunnar?" Rowdy had asked him at the party. "A cowboy who can't ride a horse for any length of time?"

"Yes I can, Gunnar told him. "Wyoming ranchers have horses out of love and tradition. But the real work gets done from a Jeep, or an ATV. An enclosed snowcat in the dead of winter."

Rowdy nodded at Gunnar's kind words.

"Being a cowboy is up here," Gunnar said, tapping on his forehead, "and here," he said, putting his hand on his heart. He was just happier than he could have imagined at having someone to talk to again about the ranch—especially after Pike's defection into the world of art, and Colton leaving the ranch for construction.

Gunnar had hoped Ash would be interested in learning the ropes of West Ranch, but he seemed to be leaning towards business.

Anyway, he was preoccupied, and rightly so, with the passing of his grandmother.

Ridge wasn't even pretending to be all that interested in ranch operations any longer.

But Rowdy West was a dyed-in-the-wool cowboy from the West Ranch in Montana—a ranch that was grand in its day, but was now history. Just a place to hang a hat for Rowdy and Gray—the last Wests standing north of Wyoming.

Rowdy had a slight limp, but didn't let that slow him down. He could hardly wait to see the four corners of the West property, including the horses, the cattle, and the bison. He wanted to see the barns and the other outbuildings, and feel the adrenaline coursing through his veins that could only come from a living, breathing ranch.

"I feel like a kid on Christmas morning," Rowdy had told Gunnar over coffee.

"Well let's go see what Santa brought," Gunnar replied with a kindred smile. "If we hurry, there's a herd of elk grazing in the basin that we can spot. And the men are tagging calves today—we'll want to see some of that."

Clapping Gunnar on the back, Rowdy smiled a tall, handsome grin and made his way for the door.

Ridge indulged in sleeping a few hours longer than usual, but figured he could get away with it as the guest of honor from the night before. His plan was to have coffee, then grab a few boxed lunches for he and Ash and drive towards town.

He was happy to hear complete silence in the house by the time he ventured into the kitchen—he didn't want to talk about his run-in with the law, and knew that someone was going to bring it up eventually.

"Looks like it's just you and me this morning," Ridge scratched Gunnar's dog Jet behind the ears and exhaled with relief as he made his way to the coffee pot, walking a bit stiffly with his sore leg.

"And me," Kat spoke from the table. She was sitting quietly with her coffee cup, and a small plate with a fried egg and a piece of toast.

Ridge jumped in surprise, then smiled at her.

"Can I fix you breakfast, Dad?" Kat asked.

"Naw, but thanks," he said. "Coffee is enough this morning. I'm still full from that second piece of cake last night." Ridge brought his cup to the table, then kissed Kat lightly on top of her head. "Thank you for the lovely birthday party."

Kat smiled.

Whatever deficiencies she felt at having her own father abandon her and her mother so many years ago, Ridge, she knew, was trying his best to make up for. The patriarch of the family poured his heart and soul into fathering his clan, and making sure all was well for the growing number of Wests on his ranch.

"It was a great night," Kat said. "One you nearly missed."

A shadow of a frown passed over Ridge's face, but he quickly recovered and let out a small laugh. "Aw, they let me out for good behavior."

"I'm a little curious about how you landed in jail," Kat said. "But I'm more concerned with what you did to your leg. Last night I noticed you limping more as the night went on."

Ridge frowned again. "Not much gets past you, does it, Dr. West?"

"Not when it comes to my family," she answered with a smile. "What are your plans today?"

Ridge was happy that Kat was changing the subject.

"I'm going to head to town and check in with Ash," he said. "Take him lunch."

"Perfect," Kat said, handing him a slip of paper. "You have an appointment with the orthopedic specialist at the hospital at one o'clock."

Ridge took a sip of his coffee while he measured his reply.

"Are you asking, or are you telling?"

"Oh, I'm *telling*," Kat told him in no uncertain terms.

Lying at Ridge's feet, Jet lifted his head and whimpered.

"I hear you boy," Ridge said with his hand on Jet's head. "Old men and old dogs. We just get told what to do."

CHAPTER 34

"*L*ooks like a pulled tendon, Mr. West."

The renowned surgeon was gently turning Ridge's knee, while gazing at an x-ray on a light screen. Ridge looked too, but couldn't make out a thing.

That's why he gets the big bucks, Ridge thought to himself as the doctor left the room. He was glad that the growing town had such good medical care, thanks to the board's insistence on hiring the best.

How he had come to get a last-minute appointment with the head of orthopedics was a mystery to Ridge—he was sure there was a wait list a mile long.

Maybe it was because his name was on the hospital, and the town.

Most likely it was because his daughter-in-law was a big shot department head of infectious diseases. It was a cause for celebration when the board was able to hire her away from her job in Chicago.

And just in time.

Kat had only been in West Gorge for a few weeks when the deadly virus swept through Wyoming and through the town—thanks to a busload of tourists carrying the germs with them wherever they went. She had to make the tough decision to shut down the medical center wing and with it, his eldest son Gunnar.

He smiled to think of how hopping mad his son must have been. Gunnar hated being in the hospital for more than a minute, on account of memories of his mother's illness.

Ridge understood, but didn't share the same associations. Thinking of Randi West in the hospital brought back only warm thoughts of the tender care she received at the hands of the medical staff. Although he had to admit that the smell of the place could bring tears to his eyes if he wasn't careful.

Instead, he chose to look around him and see all the good that was coming out of the West Gorge Medical Center.

Why, Kat, for one.

Gunnar's week inside the hospital walls forced him to make peace with Randi's passing, and caused him to take a closer look at the blind date he'd written off. Once he let his guard down, he fell hard for Kat, and she for him.

Now they had each other, which made Ridge's heart swell with happiness. And together they'd given him his first grandchild—little baby Willow. She was a great delight to everyone on the ranch.

Gunnar had also come home from the hospital with Ash Gibson, who was now Ash West. Ridge's own son. The young boy was a young man now, growing up with integrity and learning to set aside his own painful past. Which is all Ridge wanted. He had a bright future ahead of him, Ridge knew.

Ridge gingerly slipped his jeans and boots back on as he waited for the doctor's return.

Looking out the window, he watched the construction of the Randi West Cancer Center next door. The building would take another eight or nine months to complete. Hopefully they could get the exterior finished, then work exclusively on inside spaces during the long harsh winter.

Once the lobby was completed, Pike's beautiful portrait of his mother would have prominence.

The hospital board had been putting together recommendations for the new staff, and Ridge was pleased that the community would have this resource.

"Here's a prescription for inflammation, and a referral for physical therapy," the doctor said, coming back into the exam room. "In the meantime, no ladders, no sports, and no exertion."

Ridge thanked him, then privately let his shoulders slump. He had wanted to help Ash pull up more of the flooring, or maybe demo the bathroom. But he'd have to settle for bringing him a sandwich and keeping the boy company.

On his way through the lobby, Ridge stopped to talk with Dr. Josh Quell, Kat's colleague.

"It's good to see you, Mr. West," the young doctor said. "I'm sorry I couldn't be at your party last night but I was on call."

"I understand," Ridge said.

"Kat is coming in later for a meeting," Josh continued. "She'll tell me all about it."

Before Ridge could say another word, Marta, who was working in the gift shop, shouted out to both of them.

"*I'll* tell you all about it," she said. "There was a lot of food, a lot of dancing, and then more food and dancing."

Ridge and Josh smiled at each other as Marta came out of the gift shop.

"Nels and I each had one of the bartender's fancy signature cocktails," she said, still talking as loudly as if the men were in the next the room, "and our son, Officer Jason Scott, had to drive us home!"

Ridge was about to comment, but Marta cut him off.

"Can you imagine that Ridge?" Marta asked with what he thought was a wicked grin. "Being put in a police car and given a ride?"

CHAPTER 35

*W*alking into Ash's bungalow, Ridge expected to hear the sounds of the scraper against tiles, or the electric sander as Ash worked the ancient dried glue off the plywood subflooring. Ash had put in his share of sweat equity since being handed the keys to the little house.

Instead, he heard the sounds of talking and laughing.

Was that a woman's voice?

"Hello," Ridge called from the living room.

"Oh hey," Ash said as he sauntered out from the little pink bathroom. He was covered with dust, and wearing his protective glasses on top of his head.

Coming out from the room behind him was indeed a woman—she was elegantly clothed in heels and a linen dress, wearing a silver necklace and matching hoop earrings. Her hair had a few silver streaks, as it fell in waves to her shoulder.

She was attractive, Ridge thought. Much older than Ash, but not quite as old as himself, he didn't think.

"Hello again," the woman said with a smile. Only then did Ridge recognize Casey Parks.

"Maam," Ridge nodded tersely. He found himself trying to stand a little taller, and straighten his sore leg, though he couldn't say why she deserved such efforts.

"I was giving my new neighbor a tour of Granny's house," Ash said innocently.

The boy had no idea how much Ridge disliked the woman, or the way she had stolen the Madison house from under him while they were both in jail.

When Casey spoke, it was as if she had no idea that she'd made an enemy of herself.

"I was telling your son not to completely renovate this cute little washroom," she said, indicating the pink bathroom. "Renters and buyers value the authentic details of the mid-century modern facilities. Plus, they were built to withstand a nuclear bomb."

She and Ash laughed at her joke.

Ridge did not.

"Is it just me," Casey asked Ridge, "or did a cold chill blow in the door with you?"

"No cold chill," Ridge said with a forced smile, "just me, with lunch for the boy."

"Well, *the boy* is doing a fine job with his renovation," Casey said. "He'll have no trouble at all turning the house into a vacation rental. And I've offered to help him with anything he needs, including sharing my knowledge and experience while he gets started."

Ridge softened. He knew that she was being gracious with Ash, and that his bad manners didn't become him or his family. His pride had been wounded, along with his leg, but he needed to put on his "big boy pants," as his daddy would say, and act nice.

"That's mighty kind of you, Casey," Ridge said with a nod. "Would you care to stay and share our lunch? There's plenty."

Ash seemed to exhale at Ridge's attempt at chivalry. The boy had been holding his breath, he realized.

"Next time, perhaps," Casey said with a nod. "I have a closing to get to now."

After she left, Ash turned to Ridge with a question on his face.

"What the heck was that all about?"

Ridge merely shrugged and took the lunch into the kitchen.

"Just me being prickly," he said. "I didn't like Casey getting the house, that's all."

Ash followed him and sat down. He was starving. "We'll get the next one," Ash said with a grin. "Speaking of which, Emily, my other neighbor next door, caught me this morning. She wants you to stop by and see her before you head back to the ranch later."

"I can do that," Ridge said. He looked at Ash, but couldn't detect that the boy knew any more than that.

As they ate their sandwiches and shared a thermos of coffee Kat brewed for them before Ridge left the ranch, he shared his news about the doctor's visit.

"I apologize for not being able to help you out more," Ridge said.

"Hey," Ash said, "I've got a birthday gift for you." He got up and brought a wrapped gift box to the table, which he handed to Ridge.

"What's this?" Ridge asked.

Ash smiled and shrugged. "Not nearly enough," he said.

Ridge opened the box to pull out a high-end polo shirt. It seemed like a strange gift, until he saw the embroidery on one side:

"WELL LOOK AT THAT, I made partner." Ridge finally spoke when he trusted his voice. "Ash West Properties—I like the sound of that. Thank you for the shirt, son."

Ash nodded.

"Thank you for the name, Dad."

Then Ash had more to say.

"Now Dad," he said, clearing his throat, "it's a *good* shirt. A well-made shirt, with lots of years left. But it has its limits."

"Oh?" Ridge looked up from the gift. *Were they talking about the shirt?*

"This shirt shouldn't be falling off of ladders, or peeking into dark windows," Ash said. "And it should definitely stay on the right side of the law. It's not only loved; it has a lot of responsibilities still."

Ridge nodded at his son's wisdom.

"It's a deal."

CHAPTER 36

"Oh wow, are you calling me—on the phone?" Liu's voice sounded genuinely surprised when she answered.

"Yes," Colton said. "This is me, calling you, on the phone."

"Why aren't you texting me?" She said with a distracted laugh. "My friends all text."

Exactly, is what Colton didn't say. He was trying to break free from this very zone, once and for all.

He couldn't see her, but suspected she was chopping vegetables at her stainless-steel island. He wished he was sitting there now, eating her food, but wanted to keep his invitation *official*, and not casual.

"Because I want to ask you on a date," he said, "and I thought it better to hear your voice. And for you to hear mine."

"Oh," Liu stopped chopping as she tried to process Colton's request. "A date?"

"Yes," he said, firmly. "It's not research. It's not a tour of the town. It's not a picnic. We're not returning banquet pans. It's a *date.*"

"A date date?"

Was she *toying* with him, he wondered? Or stalling?

"Liu," Colton tried again. "Chef Chen, I would like to take you out for an evening. And just so there's no confusion, I will pick you up, and I'll be dressed nice. You will dress nice. We will go to a nice restaurant for dinner."

"That's a lot of *nice*," she replied. "What's your objective, Colton?"

"My objective is romance," he said. "Would tomorrow be convenient?"

There was a long pause where neither spoke, but Colton wasn't going to let her off the hook. He had made himself clear, and it was up to her to answer him. And not to give her an out.

At last, Liu's voice broke the silence.

"Tomorrow would be lovely," she said before hanging up. "I will be ready at six."

THE NEXT NIGHT, Colton picked Liu up at the cook house with a bouquet of flowers in hand. She thanked him and put them in a vase of water before grabbing her evening bag—and indicating they could go.

He held the door as she got in a sporty sedan that was clean and polished.

Liu, Colton was pleased to see, was wearing a short dress and pretty summer shoes. She had obviously taken her time getting ready because she looked more beautiful than ever. Colton wore a crisp button-down shirt and jeans that were new and pressed.

She smiled when she saw him and nodded her approval.

"I'm glad you brought a sweater," he said before closing her door. "We're dining *al fresco*. And no, it's not the patio of Red's Rib Shack."

A little later, after a beautiful drive through the sagebrush lined hills, Colton turned down a gravel road towards a lake nestled in the foothills. A sign pointed towards The Lakeshore Inn. When the car stopped in front of the log lodge, two valets opened their doors and Colton came around to offer Liu his arm.

"This is fancy," she said walking in. They both looked up towards the beamed ceiling and the chandeliers. Over to one side of the lobby, a woman sat at a grand piano, filling the great room with delicate music.

Looking out the picture windows that faced the crystal-clear lake, Liu and Colton could see the shore lined with pines and aspens. On the far side of the shore, a half dozen people stood in the water with fly fishing rods, majestically flicking the long lines into the lake.

"This way Mister West, Miss Chen," the maître d said, and led them to a candlelit table on the surprisingly modern terrace, lined with clear glass walls for an unobstructed view. As they walked, Colton placed his hand lightly on the small of Liu's back, which sent shock waves of desire up and down her spine.

"You smell really good," she whispered to him as they reached their lakeside location, and he pulled the chair out for her.

Minutes later, over glasses of wine, Colton said, "you look beautiful tonight, Liu."

For once, Liu didn't have a deflection. She opened her mouth to make a comment, he thought, but changed her mind.

Colton watched her as they ordered and began eating, waiting for her to try and make a joke, or turn the night into something much more casual. He knew this was her defense mechanism, but hoped it would be difficult in such an elegant setting.

Liu settled into her chair and studied the menu, nodding with approval. She opted for the sea scallops and risotto—a dish she claimed few chefs could actually pull off with any success.

"I'll have what she's having," Colton told the waiter as he closed his menu. "She's the boss."

They both took another sip of their wine and turned to gaze at the lake. The setting sun cast deep shadows from the pine trees. An eagle swooped over the water, searching for fish. And a few boaters began coming in off the lake, and docking near the lodge.

Liu slipped her arms into her sweater, with Colton jumping up to help her.

"Okay, now what's all this about?" She asked him with her own eagle eye.

"As I said on the phone, Liu, it's a date."

"With the objective of romance," she said.

"Correct," he said.

"Leading to...?"

Colton smiled at her question. She was so beautiful, and so nosey. So analytical about the mysteries of life and love—she wanted to jump ahead to the last page in the book; fast-forward to the ending of the movie.

"I think that if we give our relationship a chance," Colton said, "then one of these nights we might find ourselves falling in love."

Liu watched him as he spoke, and sipped her wine. Colton couldn't tell if she was pleased, or skeptical, or what.

"I was afraid of that," she said.

CHAPTER 37

"*It's* time I told you the secret I have been keeping, Colton," she said. "You see, there's a... man, in China, that my family would like me to go and meet—his name is Bo."

Colton was silent as his heart began mud-sliding into the pit of his stomach. He couldn't believe that the Chens would arrange Liu's marriage to a stranger, not in this day and age. Not when he was right here.

"But you're not going, are you?" he asked, praying she wasn't going.

"I am going, in one week," Liu said simply.

Colton felt lightheaded, as though someone had hit him over the head.

"I don't understand," he said. And he didn't. Why would Liu kiss him, and dance with him—go on dates with him, if she was marrying another man?

She must have sensed his pain and confusion.

"I owe you an apology, Colton," Liu said quietly. "I have treated you badly."

He let her continue.

"I know that I will not love Bo; I may never love him," she said. "So when you came along, I wanted to *feel* love, and desire, for once in my life. It was very selfish of me to use you this way, and I am deeply ashamed."

He was astounded at her confession.

Looking across the table, he saw unshed tears about to spill, and handed Liu a handkerchief.

She motioned it away angrily.

"I don't deserve to cry!" She shouted to him in an agonized whisper, fighting back tears. "You are good, and I used you."

"You used me..." Colton said, "...to feel love."

She nodded, miserably.

"So, Liu," Colton continued, "you're saying that you love me."

"Of course I love you," she said. "I didn't think that was ever in doubt. But it doesn't make a difference to my family. They tell me I will grow to love a stranger someday."

Colton was elated, and confounded, and frustrated with Liu's confession.

"You're saying it's easier to fly to China and marry a man you've never met than to tell

your family you love me?" Colton tried to keep the emotion from his voice, but was hurt, and more than a little bit frightened at the thought of losing Liu.

"They aren't stupid, Colton," Liu said as gently as possible. "They see our feelings, but they think... you don't understand the bonds of family. And because of that, our marriage would be built on shaky ground. We'd be *duìmiàn*. Opposite."

Colton was stunned, not for the first time that evening.

How could the Chens possibly think that he didn't understand bonds, especially after coming to Ridge's birthday party? If anything was a testament to love, it was his own family.

"Liu, I've jumped through hoops to get it right," Colton said. "I took off the shoes. I put on the shirt. I opened my hands. I closed up the four pears and put them back in the car."

"Colton, this is not about rules. Their concerns transcend rules."

141

"And you agree with their concerns," Colton stated more than asked.

The two sipped their coffee and picked at their crème Brule while weighing their next words.

"Let me try again," Liu said at last. "You *have* a family, Colton, but do you know how to depend on them—and even more, are you allowing them to depend on you?"

"I… I don't really know," he said, truthfully.

"It's important in my family—to be intertwined this way."

Colton listened and tried to comprehend.

"I know I'm independent. And I sometimes come off as being more American than Chinese," Liu said, "but I value the Yin and Yang of family."

"We fit together, Liu," Colton said. "We make each other happy."

"Colton," Liu said, "Yin and Yang is not that two people fit together —we're more complex than mere puzzle pieces. Yin and Yang is how people reshape and mold themselves to fit into each other's lives. Our willingness to fill gaps and voids, and *bend* towards each other."

"Please Liu, give me time," Colton said. "I'm trying to really and truly understand. Because…"

"Don't say it," Liu said, holding her finger up as if to shush his lips. Her eyes glistening with unshed tears. Then she reached across the table and grabbed his hand with her own small one, holding him tight as they turned to gaze at the lake.

CHAPTER 38

*W*alking Liu to her porch and front door after their dinner, she fell into Colton's arms with all the heartbreak and confusion he knew she felt. This normally brave, take-charge woman was crushed by fear and sadness. Liu didn't want to disappoint her family, nor did she want to turn away from the love Colton was offering her.

It broke his heart to see her torn in two.

All Colton could do was wrap his arms around her and hold her tight. As she buried her face into his chest, drinking in his warmth and strength, he kissed the top of her silky hair, and nuzzled her while gently swaying back and forth.

He wanted her to feel safe as well as adored. But until he knew what their future would hold, their lingering kisses would have to wait. If she was to be another man's wife, Colton concluded, he would honor Liu and the Chens by stepping back. Though it was the hardest thing he'd ever done.

Colton wanted to be just as brave as Liu, but he was determined to fight for her if he could.

With Liu standing on the cook house porch, tears welling up in her eyes, he began walking to his car. Then he gave the parting words he knew he would always regret not saying.

"Just so there's no question, Liu; no *cultural* misunderstanding," Colton said, standing in the sagebrush under a sky full of stars, "my heart is yours for the taking. My future is yours, if you want to share it with me. My home is yours. All that I have, Chef Liu Chen, is yours. Because with or without your permission, I have fallen in love with you."

Liu brought her hand to her lips, but didn't speak.

"Make no mistake," he went on, walking a few paces backwards, "I am not a nut. I'm not just a friend. I want to be your husband."

When she still didn't speak, Colton continued.

"You are bossy and you are beautiful," he said, "and I want you to be my wife."

Colton took a few steps and grabbed onto the handle of his car door, then turned around to face her one more time. She couldn't see that he had un-spilled tears of his own by this point—but maybe she could hear it in his voice.

"Our future is in your hands, Liu," he called out to her. "I will respect whatever road you take. But I won't be coming back here."

With that, he got into his car and drove off. He didn't look in the rearview mirror. If he had, he would have a hard time not turning back as Liu doubled over in grief, and ran into the house.

One week.

Colton had just a few days to convince Liu and the Chens that he was more than a *tasty bite*—that he was ready to be Liu's main course.

He knew he could make her happy. Hadn't he jumped through hoops to wear the right colors, and learn the correct gestures? If the Chens only objection was his relationship with his own family, he could remedy that.

What do they need from you? Liu had asked this, and he didn't have an answer.

· · ·

THE NEXT DAY, Colton pushed Liu's departure from his mind, and tried to focus on his own family—it was the only way he'd get through the day.

Quickly, he found out about his dad's leg injury, and how Ridge had been helping Ash renovate the bungalow. Why hadn't he thought to help Ash himself? He and Ash had been the closest to each other when Gunnar brought him home to the ranch—Colton mentored him and laughed with him as the little brother he'd always wanted to have.

And now, Ash was himself working through a lot, both literally and figuratively. He had just lost his grandmother, and inherited her house. Colton knew he should have been stopping by all along to give Ash an hour of his time here and there, or just to check in.

What about Gunnar? Both he and Pike, and even Ridge, had left their oldest brother holding the bag at the ranch while they moved on to other pursuits. Without finding out how they could help ease the transition.

Pike seemed to have everything under control—a new bride, a new home, and a new painting studio. But maybe, just maybe, Pike could use his brothers' support and encouragement. It was a brave new world for the former cowboy.

Head in hand, Colton pondered these things. Even if helping his family more didn't lead to Liu's love, it was a good path and would keep him occupied. But it felt counterintuitive to spend what little time he had left with his own people, instead of Liu and her family.

Considering her impending trip, he wasn't even sure if Liu would go out on another date with him, or if he should even ask—the last date hadn't had the desired result, Colton knew. Sure, he had gently kissed her goodnight on the cheek, and held her hand. But there was a sadness about her—a heaviness—that dates weren't supposed to have.

Liu seemed resigned to the fact that she was leaving her free will behind, and her decision to follow her own heart by flying to China. There, she would come face to face with her destiny, according to her family's wishes, and wishes of the "aunties."

This was a Liu Colton didn't want to know. A Liu he wouldn't recognize.

CHAPTER 39

"$\mathcal{L}$iu has a trip planned," Kat said casually to Gunnar while they were having coffee a few days later. "I knew about it when she came on board. Her mother and grandparents are going to stay at the cook house in her absence, and fill the void."

Colton, who just happened to be walking to the coffee pot when the topic came up, kept his back to Gunnar and Kat while eavesdropping. It deflated him to hear the two talking so casually about a topic that crushed him to his core—but they weren't being insensitive. The two had no idea what had transpired between he and Liu.

"Maybe they can help with Willow if they have a spare minute," Gunnar said with a smile.

"Maybe. Willow loves the Chens," Kat responded. "It was really cute to see how they all took to each other."

"I'll have some time this afternoon to spell you with the baby," Gunnar offered. "Rowdy offered to make the rounds on the ranch today."

Kat raised her eyebrows at this. "You're not going to want him to leave," she said.

"Funny you should say that," Gunnar smiled, and kissed Kat on his way out the door.

Colton sat down at the table with his coffee and toast. Kat took a long look at him as she finished up her own breakfast.

"You look miserable," she stated, simply.

"That's about right," he agreed.

"Don't give up hope, Colton," Kat said softly.

Colton knew that unlike some women, his sister-in-law didn't hand out frivolous "atta-boys." If there was a reason to hope, and Colton desperately wanted something to grasp onto, he knew she wouldn't string him along.

"Why should I hope, Kat?" He asked.

"Because I saw the way she watched you—at the party. And I saw the look in her eyes when you asked her to dance," Kat said with a sad smile.

Colton couldn't help but smile himself at the recollection.

"No, Colton," Liu had repeatedly said throughout the evening, "I am working."

But with only a few dances left, he could tell that her resolve was weakening.

"Please dance with me Liu," he said again, reaching for her with his arms and pleading with his eyes. "I can't help but notice that your graceful hands are empty now." And like a miracle, she gave in to him. Flying into his arms with the most radiant grin he'd ever seen.

If only her family knew how wonderful she had felt while in his arms, they would never allow her to settle for a lesser love, he thought.

Lost in these images, toast growing cold, Colton forgot for a moment that Kat was still sitting beside him. When he looked up, her mouth was hanging open as she stared, wordlessly.

"Oh... my... goodness," Kat said at last, shaking her head slowly. "You've got it bad."

"Thank you," he said, "for reminding me about my dance with Liu. I don't think tiger mama liked it very much, but it does give me hope."

Kat nodded. She agreed that Ling was not happy with Liu's display of glee as she danced with Colton. But she also understood, and grimaced at his unflattering label.

"Listen, Colton," Kat said as she stood up to clear her dishes. "Every good mom, every good parent is a *tiger mama,* someday you'll find out for yourself. But Ling is also very wise. And fair, I believe."

"I'd like to think so," Colton said.

"Ling wants what's best for her daughter," Kat said. "I pray that's you."

CHAPTER 40

"I've got a few hours before I have to check back in with my men," Colton said to Ash. The two stood in the bungalow kitchen following Ash's tour. "What can I help you with?"

"Wow, okay," Ash thought quickly. "I have to get all the old appliances outside—the utility company is coming to recycle them. That's one job I didn't know how I would do myself."

"Then let's do it together," Colton said with a smile and an eager clap of his work gloves.

Ash grinned broadly.

"And next time, little brother," Colton said, "just ask."

Colton and Ash worked together to maneuver the stove and refrigerator out of their tight spaces, and then down the steps and onto the driveway for pick-up. Next, they took the bi-fold doors off the laundry closet and did the same with the old washer and dryer.

As they worked side by side, they talked about Ridge and the weather, and all manner of topics, laughing together the way they used to on the ranch.

"That was easy," Ash said when they were done, and confessed that he'd built the task up in his mind as nearly impossible.

"What's next?" Colton asked with a grin.

"Lunch!" Ash exclaimed. "I'm starving. You?"

"Always," Colton said. "Reds for ribs?"

"Yep, and I'm buying," Ash said.

"I should hope so," Colton teased, clapping Ash affectionately on the back as they walked towards the truck.

Next door to the bungalow, Ash's neighbor, Miss Emily, wiped away a tear as she watched the two together. She marveled at how the good Lord had looked out for the boy, knowing his mother was a dead-beat, and his granny wasn't long for the world.

She would have taken Ash in herself, but she knew she also needed to slow down. That's why she spoke with Ridge West a few days before, and asked him to purchase her little house.

"I'm sorry you lost out on the Madison house," she had told Ridge. "Though I'm a firm believer in the free market, I have a soft spot for the underdog."

Emily went on to tell Ridge that her son finally convinced her to move in with his family. They'd be arriving in about a week to help her pack, and had a little suite waiting for her, and a garden in dire need of her attention and wisdom. She wanted to have her affairs in order before she left West Gorge.

She smiled to think of Ridge's gracious response and offer—it was far and above more than the house was worth, they both knew. And much more than Casey Parks could have offered.

"You're a class act," she told Ridge as they shook hands and parted ways.

"Likewise," he had responded.

FOLLOWING LUNCH, Colton dropped Ash off at the bungalow and turned towards the new subdivision being built. But before heading to check on the new houses, he turned towards Pike and Paislee's farmhouse.

"Just checking on my handiwork," he called out as he walked towards the porch minutes later. The newlyweds were sitting on their porch swing, reading the West Gorge newspaper.

"Well you're a sight for sore eyes," Paislee greeted him enthusiastically with a hug.

"I imagine that's true," Colton said, "when all you get to look at each day is Pike."

The three laughed as Pike got Colton a chair, and Paislee fetched a tray of cold iced teas. As they visited, Colton filled the two in on Ash's bungalow, and Ridge's injured leg. Then they wandered back to Pike's art studio, so Colton could take a look at the latest work.

Gazing at a new landscape Pike was working on of the gorge in springtime, Colton remarked at the beauty that surrounded them in Wyoming, and how Pike had captured its essence.

"This one!" Colton excitedly pointed to the painting, then quickly opened his hand palm side up and gestured as Liu had taught him. "I want this painting to hang in my house when I get it built. Will you save it for me?"

Pike looked taken aback, and genuinely pleased.

"I'd be honored to have one of my paintings in your house, Colton," Pike said. "Especially since your own craftsmanship is all over mine."

The brothers parted ways then, and Colton said farewell to his new sister-in-law—who glowed at the unexpected visit. *She must miss her family*, he thought.

"Give my regards to your sisters," he told Paislee, "and your parents."

"I will," Paislee said with a smile, though she had a mist in her eyes. "Pike and I will see them soon. We're going to Denver for a few weeks so my daddy can continue showing off his new son-in-law. And for my sister's celebration—she's being promoted at the bank."

Colton nodded and made a note to send flowers. Paislee's younger sisters were both beautiful, and in another life, he would have enjoyed getting to know them better. But in that other life, he hadn't known Liu Chen.

CHAPTER 41

*T*he next few days flew by in a flurry of activity for Colton, as he threw himself into the affairs of his family and their circumstances, while avoiding Liu and hers.

Leaning on his construction manager a little more, Colton took some time to accompany Ridge to a few of his physical therapy appointments, just so he could hear for himself what his dad needed to do—and not do—to heal. Ridge bristled at first, but then Colton promised they could swing by Cindy's Diner in their travels. The elder West never passed up a chance to have a burger and fries from his old friend and restaurant owner.

"I love Liu," Ridge said, innocent of Colton's feelings, "but her cooking is so... *healthy*."

"Yeah, I love her too," Colton had answered. He didn't think his dad noticed his growing friendship with Liu, and how it had turned into love.

By spending some time with his dad, Colton realized how little the two actually talked in their day-to-day life, and how much they had to catch up on. Especially now that Colton wasn't working on the ranch with Gunnar.

He filled Ridge on the plans for his home site, and said he anticipated his crew having some time in coming weeks to begin pouring the foundation.

"It's a beautiful site you picked, Colton," Ridge said. "Your mother and I talked about building a cabin there someday; a place to get away from everything. But we never did."

Ridge told his son he was glad that he was staying on the property, and wouldn't be far away.

"I know Pike is right in town," Ridge lamented, "but it feels too far at times."

Colton had to agree. He took for granted all the years when the brothers were under the same roof, even though they came and went as the ranch demanded.

Ridge also confessed to Colton that he feared Ash would want to live at the bungalow in town after he completed the renovation. One or two times, the boy had worked late in the night and had been too exhausted to drive home on the desolate ranch road.

"I'd like him to be firmly entrenched in the family, and on the ranch, before he breaks away from us," Ridge said.

Colton listened and nodded, and promised to be more mindful of the situation. He made time to stop by the bungalow nearly every day to help Ash with a project, or just to pat the kid on the back for the work he was doing.

One afternoon, he walked in without knocking and heard unusual grunts and groans coming from the little TV den. It sounded like someone was hurt, or crying. Gingerly, Colton made his way to the source, and found Ash on his knees. He was pulling up old carpeting with a vengeance, and sobbing at the same time—as if the layer of flooring was his pent-up pain, and he could peel it away with brute force.

"*Damn* them," Ash sobbed over and over, under his breath.

Ash had neglected to put on his work gloves, and his hands were red and swollen from the scratchy backing. They bled from nicks caused by the many carpet tacks.

Colton placed a hand on Ash's back, which stopped the pulling, but not the crying. He got down on the floor with the young man and held him tight until the crying stopped. When they did, Ash fell fully into Colton like a limp rag. After a few minutes, he gently helped Ash stand and walked him to his truck, locking up the little house behind him.

"Let's get you home, little brother," Colton said.

Ash didn't resist.

Before getting into the truck himself, he sent a text to Gunnar, Kat, and Ridge, asking if anyone was home, and could they be ready with a first aid kit. Maybe some aspirin.

Everyone was there, including Rowdy. Quietly watching his every move, the boy's family led him to the table where Dr. Kat took over, tenderly cleaning and dressing Ash's hands. Ridge had some pain killers and water. Gunnar had a comforting hand on the boy's shoulder, and a concerned look in his eyes. Rowdy had rustled around in the fridge and made Ash a hearty sandwich and poured him a cold soda.

Ash appeared to be in shock. He didn't resist the bandages or the aspirin. He took a few bites of the sandwich, but continued to look off into space, not meeting anyone's eyes. After a time, Ash gave his head a slight shake, then looked around at his family, gathered in the kitchen. Nodding silently, he got up and went to his room, presumably to sleep.

"He's dehydrated, exhausted, and pushing himself way to hard," Kat said. "And, I suspect he's trying to fast-track the process of grieving the loss of his grandmother by burying himself in his project."

Thankfully, Ash slept until the following day and woke up like himself again. He told his dad he was going to stay home at the ranch for a day or so and just "hang out." Ridge told him he was awfully glad Ash was taking a break.

"When you're ready," Ridge said, "we'll go back together, and take it slower."

Colton spent time with his oldest brother too. He tagged along with Rowdy and Gunnar when he could, and marveled at his cousin's love for ranching. Colton could see that Rowdy's enthusiasm was contagious. Gunnar was energized again, and excited about West Ranch operations.

And with Gray away on a training mission, Rowdy wasn't home alone on the piece of land they still owned in Montana.

Finally, Colton made opportunities to play with little Willow, and spell Kat a time or two so she could return phone calls, or work in her office. The smile that lit up the baby's face when she saw her favorite cowboy warmed his heart, and almost made him forget about missing Liu—and maybe losing her.

That is, until he allowed his mind to wander to the life he longed to build with the crazy, bossy, beautiful chef, and the children he prayed they'd have. Though it was currently just a plot of sagebrush and a few wooden stakes, he could picture that life so clearly.

Colton saw Liu padding through the living room, owning every inch of the kitchen, and sitting with him under the stars at night.

When these thoughts took over the distance became unbearable.

Looking at his phone for the millionth time, he could see that she still hadn't called or sent him a message. By his calculations, she would be leaving the next day for China.

Could he see her just one more time?

CHAPTER 42

"*M*ister Chen," Colton said when he arrived at the cook house. Tao was sitting on the front porch, under the shade of the trees. The younger man stood with his hat in hand, and bowed slightly to Liu's grandfather.

"Ah, Mister West," Tao said, "please join me. I am enjoying the view of the mountains from this vantage point, and I would like some company."

Colton was stunned for a moment. He'd never heard two words coming out of the elder man, except for the baby talk he exuberantly spoke when Willow was around. Why had he assumed Tao only spoke Chinese?

"I came to see Liu," Colton said as he sat down on the porch. How many times had he sat here next to Justice? More than he could count. Yet, today he was without the sense of familiarity he had in the past.

"Yes," Tao said simply. "Sit, please."

There was afternoon shade on the porch of the cook house, thanks to a small grove of aspen trees that had matured in the years since they were first planted, thirty years before.

The old camp cook had been happy with his folding chairs, and a rusty glider. But when he left, Kat had the little porch re-stained, then added an outdoor table and chairs set made from teak. This is where Tao sat, and where Colton joined him. Both men, it seemed, were glad to be out of the mid-day Wyoming sun.

"One generation plants the trees," Tao gestured to the aspens, "another generation enjoys the shade."

Colton smiled and nodded at the wisdom.

After a few moments of silence, Colton looked over to the side of the house. He was about to point, but then remembered his manners and held out his open hands.

"Liu should have a garden," Colton said, "over there, I think. Near the water spigot." He dropped his hands, but continued to look.

Tao looked too, and nodded in agreement.

"I should dig the land up this Autumn," Colton continued, "and build a pergola over the garden, for diffused light that won't burn the new shoots. Then it will be ready to plant in the Spring."

Tao nodded again.

"I'll put up a fence, to keep the critters out," Colton said.

Tao nodded and smiled. "Yes, a *tall* fence," he said. Both Colton and Tao knew that it would take a tall fence to keep the mule deer from eating the growing greens.

Now it was Colton's turn to nod again.

"Is she..." he began, and faltered. "Can I please see Liu, Mister Chen?"

Tao smiled and nodded, which Colton wanted to take as a *yes*, but his next words did not match this action.

"Liu has gone away," he said simply.

"Away," Colton repeated, trying not to sound alarmed though he was. She had not mentioned leaving early for her trip. "I thought I had more time."

"Tonight you will sleep under the same moon, from far away," Tao said.

Colton felt like he'd been punched in the gut by the soft-spoken words of Liu's grandfather. He tried to maintain his composure, and mirror the countenance of Tao. But his heart was breaking at the thought of her leaving for China to meet the match her family had set up.

While his heart and emotions twisted and turned, Colton struggled not to break the acceptable confines of conversation with Tao. He willed himself to remain still, even though everything inside urged him to storm through the little house and demand answers of the gentle people inside.

Colton took steady shallow breaths, and calmed his heart. At last, he dared to speak.

"She went... to China." He said in as steady a voice as he could.

Tao did not speak for a long while. When he did, Colton was again surprised, and disheartened at the disconnect, and slow cadence of the answer.

"As a small boy, I did not see my father for many days in a row," Tao said gently. "My father worked underground, in the coal mines. The railroad needed many men who were small enough to fit in the tight quarters. Men who were strong enough to hammer away at the rock-hard walls of the earth. Men who were hungry enough to work the long hours necessary to feed the railroad and its growth."

Colton closed his eyes in discouragement, but remained silent.

"At last, when my father had a few hours with our family," Tao said, "he was tired, but overjoyed. He told me, *you are my strength and my weakness.*"

Not wanting to seem rude, Colton nodded, but did not understand his story, or what it had to do with him.

"Children are what we work for, Colton," Tao said, causing Colton to snap to attention. "Liu needed her father, and he needed to be with his daughter. She has gone to Silicon Valley to be with Zhang for a time."

Relief flooded Colton like the rushing waters of the West River through the gorge. She hadn't gone to China, as he feared! In spite of himself, and the show of emotion he was trying to avoid, he dropped his head in his hands and squeezed his eyes shut.

"Thank God," he muttered under his breath.

Tao remained silent, and Colton thought he could make his exit. But then the older man spoke again, holding him captive.

"There is a Chinese saying, *Shuǐmǎn zé yì,*" Tao said softly to Colton, though not looking directly at him. "The water is full... but it overflows."

Colton exhaled and tried to measure his response. The Chen family, he knew, did not favor rushed conversations. He would have to pay attention to find out what wisdom Tao had in store for him.

"Okay," he said in response, nodding his head slowly. "Ah," Colton ventured, "like, *what comes up must come down,* maybe."

"Perhaps," Tao said at last, unconvinced.

Just then, Chun came out to the porch carrying a tray with a pot of tea and two cups. She must have heard Colton's voice. Both men thanked the grandmother as she poured tea for them, but Tao also spoke to her in Chinese. At that, Chun went into the house to retrieve a third cup and saucer, which she placed on the tray before returning to the house.

"*Shuǐmǎn zé yì,*" Tao said again as he picked up the teapot and poured into the third cup, until it reached the rim and flowed over into the saucer. Colton's instinct was to reach out and grab the pot, sure that Tao needed help, but he was glad he stopped himself. Tao was in full control.

"The water overflows like this extra cup of tea," Tao said as he set the pot down, and gestured towards the full cup which overflowed into the saucer. "Things must reverse when they reach their extremes."

Colton nodded but frowned. He was desperate to understand what Liu's grandfather was saying, but felt helpless. It was a puzzle he would never solve, it seemed.

Tao took another sip of his tea, and gestured to the overflowing cup.

"You... are like this cup," the elder man said quietly. "The tea... is your reliance on yourself, Colton. It has reached its extreme. If you are to understand Liu and our ways, your self-reliance must reverse."

Colton tried hard to comprehend.

"As for Liu, Tao continued, "she has her own tea that overflows her cup."

Silent again, Tao sipped his tea.

Colton did the same. He was comfortable sitting with Tao, lost in his own thoughts. *Had he come to the end of himself—had he been too self-sufficient, and pushed his own family away?*

That seemed to be a habit he'd developed since his mother died. Maybe he had been too quick to flash his smile and his good-natured shrug, and tell everyone that he was okay. But maybe, just maybe, he wasn't okay.

He had been trying harder to engage with his family, and show them they could count on him. But perhaps Tao was saying that he could never really understand the Chen family until he learned to depend on them, too. More than he ever had. After all, asking Liu to change her dependence on her family was unfair if he wasn't willing to make his own concessions.

That was the Yin and Yang.

Like any couple with such diverse backgrounds, they would have to meet in the middle to have a fighting chance. And Colton wanted to have a fighting chance to win Liu's heart more than he wanted anything else in the world.

So while she was wrestling with her own overflowing tea cup, he would take Tao's advice.

Standing to face Tao, Colton bowed in deep respect to the elder Mister Chen, thanking him for his wisdom and his time before striding to his truck.

He hoped he hadn't made any mistakes.

CHAPTER 43

Watching the young man drive away, Tao was struck by the cowboy's crestfallen face. His own father, and his grandfather, had admonished him to keep his family in the community—in other words, be sure that Chinese marry Chinese.

If Liu should marry an American, he would surely feel like a failure in this regard.

But his ancestors weren't here to see the love on Colton's face, or the broken heart the cowboy wore on his yellow shirtsleeve for his granddaughter Liu.

They couldn't see the love that existed between the cowboy and baby Willow—it was a pure joy that would melt even the hardest heart, and raised Colton's stock in Tao's eyes. Knowing the next generation of children would be loved in such a way was priceless to the grandfather.

As the older man sipped his tea under the shade of Aspen trees, Tao had to wonder how successful he would feel pushing Liu to marry for tradition, rather than for love.

Times had certainly changed since the news circled the globe in the 1840s that there was gold in California—in America—and fortunes could be made.

China was not immune to the gold fever. Within ten years, 25,000 Chinese immigrants had moved to California. To a land called *gam saan*, or Gold Mountain. Tao's own family was among the hopeful. And why not? Chinese travelers had been crisscrossing the world for long centuries, making new homes in faraway lands.

Chinese merchants, bankers, miners, and artists established homes in countries from Polynesia to Peru—bringing their families with them and building thriving communities.

In America, however, life was much harder.

For many Chinese immigrants, the gold mountain was a disappointment. An illusion. Mining was uncertain work, and the gold fields were littered with penniless and hostile prospectors.

Work was scarce, and new arrivals barely survived, let alone got rich.

They were cut off from their families. With no source of money, few immigrants could pay for their wives and children to make the long voyage from China, and many were without the money needed to return home.

Somehow, Tao's ancestors survived in a land that did not welcome them, even as the dream of gold faded. They made their way to Wyoming to work in the mines for the railroad. And even with hostility, persecution, and great prejudice against the Chinese, the Chen family aligned with the small number that remained, and grew.

In Tao's heart, he knew that sticking together with the Chinese was safe, and good. And allowing Liu to dilute this tenant was frightening.

As the elder of the family, it was his responsibility to see that Liu understood the importance of what she was about to do. And yet, a long and successful union was important, too. Divorce had become all too common in the Chinese community. Tao wondered about the marriage of Liu and Bo—a man nobody knew. An unhappy marriage would also bring shame into the family. It would extinguish Liu's bright light.

Exhausted by the quandary, Tao closed his eyes to rest. An

outsider might think he was lazy, drinking tea and napping in the shade all afternoon. But pondering these monumental things was a job nobody else had volunteered for.

CHAPTER 44

A short while after visiting with Tao, after having sent another message to his family—his entire family—he sat at the kitchen table and waited to see how they would respond.

Gunnar was the first to storm in with cousins Gray and Rowdy in tow. "Where's the fire, Colton?" Gunnar demanded to know as the men sat down at the table. Kat came in from her home office and looked at Colton with concern.

Willow was napping in her crib.

"Is everyone all right?" Ridge came in from outside, followed closely by Ash, who had left his AP class early after getting Colton's message. He dropped his backpack on the large island, and got a glass of water before sitting down with the family.

The front door opened again, and Pike and Paislee came rushing into the kitchen.

"We came as soon as we could, Colton," Pike said with a frown on his face. "What's this family meeting all about?"

Colton looked up at his family with eyes glistening—for once he didn't try to hide his emotions behind his gregarious façade. He had never in his life expressed anything to them that wasn't carefree, and the temptation was there now to diffuse the concern with a joke, or a laugh. But that wouldn't get him to where he needed to be for Liu.

"First of all," Colton said, looking around, "I want to say that I miss my mother more than I've ever let on to any of you."

He watched as everyone's face softened and crumpled, respectively.

"I also want to say," Colton continued, "and I may never say this again, but I love each of you more than I've ever expressed. You all are my *good fortune*, as much as a rag tag group of cowboys can possibly be."

Now, tears were threatening to spill from Kat and Paislee's eyes, and Ridge's chin was quivering.

"But the real reason I called you," Colton said, "is that there's something I want to do, but I can't possibly do it alone. I desperately need you, and your help—and I need it now."

Not skipping a beat, the West clan nodded and gathered around the young cowboy has he laid out his plans.

FOR THE NEXT FEW DAYS, Casey Parks was unable to scare up Ash or Ridge at the bungalow—neither were to be found. When popping by the Madison house, her newest acquisition, she saw Miss Emily outside her own little house watering the garden, and went to speak with her.

"Oh, I haven't seen the boys," she told Casey. "Ash mentioned an emergency project they were all working on—*all* the Wests—and told me he'd be back when it was finished."

Casey Parks wished she knew what they were up to. Since meeting Ridge in jail, and getting to know Ash, she felt a part of their world, somehow. And enjoyed the sensation.

At the hospital, Josh Quell showed up on his day off to cover for Kat, who said there was a family emergency. She needed a few days off.

"It's not a *medical* emergency, Josh," she told him, "just one of those unavoidable things that come up in big families—you know all about that, I suppose, more than I do."

Josh smiled at the conversation. His own big family would be arriving in a few months from Iowa for his wedding.

"Just let me know if there's anything else you need, Kat," he told her amiably. Josh had hit the jackpot with Kat as a boss, though he wasn't so sure at the beginning. Not when she was tottering around during an epidemic on impractically high heels, wearing a skimpy dress.

But since then, she had grown into her position. And she had also grown in grace and confidence, allowing him to step into a greater leadership role as she took a few steps back—something not every doctor's ego would allow them to do.

Over at West Gorge Woods, Colton's second in charge was stepping up and giving orders in his boss' absence. Colton said he'd need a few days off, but expected construction to continue. Not only that, he expected deadlines to be met, and for all inspections to pass. If anyone working for West Development had a notion that the young easygoing boss was going to be a pushover, they'd have another think coming.

The Wests were keeping Red and his team at Red's Rib Shack busy with large orders, for delivery. But they didn't want the food sent to the ranch house, or even to the pavilion.

"*Where* do they want this food to go?" Red's wife Jackie had asked. She didn't trust that she'd heard right the first time they phoned. "Well I'll be," she exclaimed once they clarified the location.

Even Daisy Shire from the gallery in town was affected by the super-secret West family project. Paislee called to cancel their Arts and Culture Center meeting at the last minute.

"I can't say anymore just yet, Daisy," Paislee said on the phone from Pike's truck. "The whole family is going to be tied up for a few days. But we will reconvene very soon."

Ridge didn't have such an easy time cancelling his physical therapy appointment, and had to make all sorts of promises to his therapist to get back in her good graces. "Yes," he said, "I will do my stretches, and I won't exert my leg. And yes… yes… I promise not to cancel again."

Ridge was dutifully sitting in a folding chair in the shade overseeing the project, which had only taken days, instead of weeks, with everyone's help. He shook his head in wonder at what they completed as a team—as a family.

Colton came and sat with him, handing Ridge a cold bottle of water.

"I don't know how I'll ever thank everyone," Colton said, looking over at the finished structure. Paislee, in torn jeans, was placing the silk cushions she had ordered for a rush delivery—that girl knew how to get things done. On one of the cushions, Willow sat playing happily with her toys.

Meanwhile, Pike and Gunnar were sanding and staining, while Kat and Rowdy used their shovels to plant the exotic landscape plants around the edge. Gray and Ash hung the lanterns and tea lights.

"That's the point of family," Ridge said. "You don't need to thank anyone."

Colton nodded at his father's words.

"Colton," Ridge said slowly and thoughtfully, "you've always been so easy-going, like a 'set it and forget it' kind of guy. But maybe I've forgotten you for too long. I'm ashamed to say that. Your mama would have my hide."

"I miss mama," Colton said. "But just look at her legacy."

CHAPTER 45

"What..." Liu got out of the car, and looked over at her father, who had also gotten out.

He merely smiled and nodded for her to walk with him.

A week before, Liu had arrived on the doorstep of his California hotel suite feeling crumpled and heartbroken; bruised in places that could not be seen. She sobbed in his arms, and stayed in a trance for days until she was ready to confess her deep and forbidden love for the cowboy.

She asked her father to forgive her disrespect, but told him she wasn't yet ready to fly to China. But she would work hard towards becoming stronger, so she could fulfill her obligations.

This emotion was uncharacteristic for Liu, or any of the Chens. In a hushed voice, Zhang spent days conferring in phone conversations with Ling, and his parents. In the evenings, at Zhang's insistence, he and Liu sampled the area restaurants, and took long walks in the many parks. Sometimes they talked, and other times they enjoyed companionable silence.

She is broken, like my own heart, Zhang whispered to Ling.

We made a mistake letting her work at the ranch, Ling whispered back.

And when he had completed his work deadline, Zhang made plane reservations to bring Liu back to Wyoming.

She had been surprised when her father said he was flying home with her, and surprised again when, hours later, he drove her past the cook house without stopping, or explanation.

With her face pressed against the car window, Liu had watched the landscape as it became more and more familiar. By the time her father stopped, they were still on West land, she knew. They were down by the gorge. Near Colton's...

LIU FROWNED in confusion as she walked slowly towards a structure, which sat in front of the winding creek, next to the site of Colton's new home. It looked like a pavilion of sorts, and Liu could smell the new wood. Along the path leading up to it, sawdust mingled with the sagebrush and rocks.

Only when her eyes adjusted to what was inside the pavilion—both her family *and* the West family sitting on cushions, in front of an expansive low-setting table—did she realize it was a tea house.

"Oh my stars," Liu said to no one at all, mouth gaping.

With her father behind her, Liu stopped to stare. The teak wood had simple lines, with open grid walls that allowed the breeze to come in. Above, a pitched roof curved elegantly over the eaves to block the sun and rain. Inside, Ling and Tao sat and smiled at Liu—little Willow was napping in Auntie Ling's lap.

"Welcome," Paislee came down the steps and bowed slightly at Liu. She gestured with her open hands for Liu and Zhang to follow her up the four steps. They stopped to slip off their shoes, adding them to a neat line of cowboy boots, heels and sandals, and then entered.

Paislee motioned for Zhang to walk to one side of the table and kneel at an empty space next to Ridge and Gunnar. He lovingly touched the shoulder of Ling as he walked by, and she smiled up at him.

Liu silently took in every touch; every gesture.

Paislee then motioned for Liu to walk on the other side, and kneel next to Colton. The cowboy nodded and bowed ever so slightly, but did not make direct eye contact with her.

Once Paislee went to kneel near Pike and Ash, Chun stood.

"Kāishǐ," she said in a quiet voice, *begin*, and lifted her hand in a sweeping motion.

From outside the tea house a quartet of violinists began playing softly. Their strings were in concert with the sound of the water splashing over the rocks. As Liu looked on in amazement, Chun poured tea from two separate pots, delivering the cups to each person.

Looking across the table, Liu tried to catch her mother's eye and find out what was going on. She was trembling, being so close to Colton, and was working hard to keep her composure. She hadn't heard from him, not a call or a text. She had assumed he had let her go —and why not, after the horrible way she had treated him.

Ling only smiled and nodded, as did her grandfather, confusing her all the more.

She couldn't stand it any longer. Her American upbringing warred with her Chinese countenance and her curiosity won out.

"You built a tea house, Colton!" Liu quietly exclaimed in astonishment.

"Yes, but I didn't do it alone," he answered. "My family helped me build it," he said. "Your grandfather helped me see how much I needed to rely on them more than I have."

Liu raised her eyebrows.

"It's... lovely," Liu said to Colton, without looking directly at him.

"It's a wedding gift," he said softly, "for you."

Liu inhaled sharply in surprise.

"And after speaking with your parents, I asked everybody here today to discuss bringing our two families together, through a marriage," Colton said, "between you and I."

Liu braced herself for her family's shock and anger, but instead, her father spoke.

"A marriage would be... favorable," he said.

Liu looked up in surprise. Her mother, across the table, smiled peacefully and nodded.

"A marriage would be favorable," Ridge West said next.

Liu couldn't believe her ears. One by one, each member of both families expressed their consent for her and Colton to marry—including her grandfather. But she had not heard from Chun, and couldn't bear to disappoint one so important. Surely her grandmother knew she would be breaking her commitment to marry from the homeland.

She kept her head down as Chun served a cup of tea to Colton.

Liu was the last.

Finally, Chun set a cup of tea in front of Liu and touched her lightly on the shoulder. Tears brimming in her closed eyes, head hanging low, she inhaled and thought there must be some mistake. The tea was not the usual—it had a floral scent.

Opening her eyes, she could see that her grandmother had served her the same tea she gave Kat and Paislee—the tea meant for fertility. It could only mean one thing. Chun's blessing!

Breaking into a smile, she looked over at Colton, who spoke again.

"It seems everyone in the family finds a marriage between the bride and groom favorable, but we have not yet heard from the bride," Colton said.

Liu was struck at how he referred to them as one family instead of two.

The family, he had said.

Looking around, she saw peace and love on each face and her heart swelled. Her mother lovingly stroked Willow's back as the baby slept. Ridge and Zhang talked amiably in low tones.

Surely, they had all witnessed what she was now just seeing—what man but Colton West would go to such lengths to declare his love for her, and his respect for the Chens? No other man in Wyoming, or China, or in the world would wear yellow shirts every day, or build a tea house with his brothers just to prove his love and devotion.

"What does the bride say?" Colton asked again, interrupting her thoughts.

Liu looked over at him—he was trying so desperately to respect the Asian culture by not addressing her directly, and yet, trying to propose marriage to the woman he loved.

She smiled and blushed with youth and happiness at her good fortune.

"The bride says... *yes*," Liu said quietly, barely containing a joyous laugh. "I'm going to marry a Wyoming cowboy in a Chinese tea house."

At that declaration, everyone laughed, even the Chens. Willow stirred, but didn't wake.

Colton turned his head to look at Liu, and reached up to lightly caress her shoulder. His eyes were filled with his love for her.

She knew he wanted to kiss her, but was afraid of breaking a tea house custom. This big strong cowboy was frozen in his sense of respect, and it just about broke her heart that she had almost let such a good man get away by not fighting for him, as hard as he fought for her. Liu silently vowed to love him well. And to always show more emotion than custom allowed. And to sometimes let him be the boss of her.

Looking into his eyes, Liu felt an overwhelming sense of joy, and was nearly speechless. Finally, a smile played on her lips.

"Hungry?" she asked him.

"Always," he answered.

CHAPTER 46

"*O*i, Willow, jump… that's right, jump," Tao laughed as he held the baby's hands. He was tasked with keeping the baby happy while everyone finished getting ready for the wedding ceremony. It was a sunny day in early September, and Liu would marry Colton in a small ceremony at the teahouse—*Liu's* teahouse.

As Tao held her tiny hands, Willow, on strengthening legs, jumped with glee on Liu's bed in the cook house. "For fertility, and many cousins," he said joyfully as the baby laughed.

The newlyweds would return to the cook house together after their reception at the ranch. They decided to stay in West Gorge through the fall, so Colton could complete the homes in his new development. Then the two planned on honeymooning in Asia for the month of December, starting out in Hanoi, Vietnam, for a foodie tour.

For today's ceremony, Chun had cooked the feast, with Liu's help. Just as they had cooked together for many years. But Liu insisted, respectfully, that her grandmother not trouble herself with the cake— Liu asked Cindy to attend the ceremony, and bring a cake with her, if she could.

A second reception would be held a week later in Rock Springs, for the many friends of the Chens to wish the couple good fortune in their marriage.

At last, Ling and Zhang arrived at the cook house to get the baby and the grandfather, and drive them to the tea house where Chun was waiting. The bride, who had been getting ready at the larger ranch house with Paislee and Kat, would be chauffeured by Ridge. Colton had been relegated to Pike's house, with the rest of the men. There, he withstood a barrage of teasing and advice from his brothers and cousins—tempered, no doubt, for Ash's young ears.

"Isn't it time to go?" The nervous groom asked more than once. Until finally, it was time.

With a stringed ensemble playing near the stream, the groom stood waiting in the tea house he had built to win Liu's heart. His three brothers by his side.

Glancing over, he saw the new stakes in the ground where he had increased the size of his house. He added a much larger pantry, and a studio for Liu where she could edit her blog videos. Colton also designed a sizeable guesthouse for the Chen family to stay for as long as they'd like. With any luck, if the weather held, they would get the foundation poured and the outside walls up before winter.

In the meantime, he would live with Liu in the cook house. He looked forward to sitting at her island, and not having to leave. Or pretend to have a reason to be there. Plus, he had fond memories of Liu's walk-in shower.

Shaking his head to center his thoughts, Colton turned in time to see his bride approaching the tea house on the arm of her father. She was a vision in yards of soft, buttery yellow silk that flowed behind and around her. The long dress was cinched at her tiny waist, with narrow delicate sleeves that tapered down to her beautiful hands— where Colton would soon place a wedding ring crafted from gold, diamonds, and rare jade.

Zhang guided Liu to Colton as the violins played. Her eyes were intensely focused on him, with tears that threatened to spill. Liu's full lips were red and luscious and slightly parted, as if ready for her husband's kiss.

Soon, my bride, he thought.

Colton nearly gasped at her beauty, and the handful of wedding guests murmured audibly when she made her appearance.

His throat and heart were being squeezed by the love he felt for her, and he wondered if he'd be able to say his vows, even—he was that speechless. Colton had worked so hard to prove his love to this lovely young woman who was so bossy and complex, with so many hopes and dreams of her own.

He silently vowed to love her with all his might, every day of his life. To be her friend forever and ever, as in the Chinese wedding poem being read by Ling.

STANDING NEXT TO HIM, he could see the tall mountains towering behind Liu, and knew they could never be flat. The river could never run dry. And he would never part from his beautiful, lovely wife.

END

FROM THE AUTHOR

To my readers:

Stirring Her Cowboy was a joy to write. I have the highest respect for the Chinese immigrants who overcame obstacles to build their lives in the rough and rugged American West, and Wyoming in particular. I ask you to look past any errors I may have made in the use of the Chinese language, and look to my intentions—they were kindly meant.

Please take what little glimmer of history I added to this book and then do your own reading and research to find out more. You won't be sorry.

Don't miss the next book in the Wild Wests saga. Order Her Sunset Cowboy here, to be released April, 2021.

Her Sunset Cowboy

Her shady ex left her with nothing. Now she won't let anything stand in the way of rebuilding her business. Even the handsome billionaire who keeps crossing her path.

After her lowlife ex took off with all her savings, Casey Parks has to pick herself up and rebuild—and she does so with a vengeance. Her take-no-prisoners attitude is all the fuel she needs to rebuild her Wyoming real estate empire. Until her ambition puts her in a head-on collision with Ridge West - town legend, billionaire benefactor, and major thorn in her side. As the handsome widower sets his sights on her territory, Casey pulls out all her tricks to slow him down—but for how long?

Ridge West is too far down the road for love. At least, that's what he keeps telling himself. But his heart is telling him a different story. Especially when he's anywhere near Casey Parks. She just seems to wake up parts of him that have been asleep for a long time. Even when she's out-bidding, out-maneuvering and undermining his every move. He doesn't even like Casey—he couldn't possibly be falling in love with her…could he?

Funny and heartfelt, can these enemies find their happily-ever-after together? Or will love pass them by forever?

OTHER BOOKS BY KATHY FAWCETT

Her Quarantined Cowboy

Wild Wests #1

Their blind date is a disaster, and both are happy when it's cut short. Then a quick spreading virus forces Kat to lock down the hospital—with Gunnar inside. He hates being stuck anywhere, with anyone. But Dr. Kat is the new sheriff in town, and she won't let him bend the rules in her hospital. Forced to work together, anger turns to admiration--which turns to romance. But can it last when the quarantine is over?

Drawing Her Cowboy

Wild Wests #2

Beautiful and rich, Paislee seems to have a perfect life – but she feels like she's losing herself in the smothering grip of her controlling fiancée. So when her grandmother suggests a road trip to unravel a family mystery, she jumps at the chance. She is determined to find answers, and finds more than she bargained for when she follows Pike to the old settler's barn. Trapped by a blizzard, Paislee is soon wearing a prairie dress and dining by candlelight with the cowboy who caught her imagination. Will he catch her heart, too?

Shoulder Season

Lake Michigan Lodge #1

Kay is finally renovating her lodge and her life. Now who will she share it with? In this funny uplifting tale of renovation, redemption and romance, a rustic old lodge on Lake Michigan isn't the only thing that gets a second chance.

Water Dance

Lake Michigan Lodge #2

In Book #2 of the Lake Michigan Lodge Series, can Kay's happy-ever-after survive an invasion of teenage girls?

About the Lake Michigan Lodge series

A rambling vintage tourist lodge nestled in a sunny bay on Lake Michigan is the only home wise-cracking Kay Kerby has ever known. She loves Kerby Lodge. But running it? Not so much. As far as Kay is concerned, the best season begins when the last lodger packs up their sunscreen and novelty t-shirts and goes home. Now an epic snowstorm pounds the coastline, and a blizzard of bills and taxes threaten to bury Kerby Lodge.

But the storms Kay doesn't see coming are the unpredictable Mayne brothers —a cloud of curls and attitude named Daniel and his younger brother Luke, a nomadic school teacher. After a devastating career loss, the mysterious Daniel just wants to be left alone. Kay is only too happy to oblige him. Then a freak accident and record-breaking blizzard leave them holed up together. Now the only person Kay can confide in is Luke, and he's thousands of miles away. Forced by walls of snow to face their broken dreams, Kay and Daniel set out on a journey of reclamation. In the process Kay finds herself hopelessly entangled with the Mayne brothers. One brother makes her laugh. The other just makes her crazy.

ABOUT THE AUTHOR

Kathy Fawcett is the author of sweet romantic comedy and women's fiction that will keep you smiling, crying and turning pages long past your bedtime. Kathy's funny dialogue and heartfelt stories make her a favorite with a growing number of fans. They love the true-to-life situations, happy endings and highly satisfying sequels. Kathy transports readers to the surf, sand and snow of charming Lake Michigan towns, as well as the windswept mountains of Wyoming.

Home is Michigan, where Kathy worked for years as an advertising writer. She met and married her husband Steve while students at Northern Michigan University, and he introduced her to his home state of Wyoming. Together, they reside near the Great Lakes with their bossy cat Sam, and are surrounded by grown children, growing grandchildren, and towering pine trees. Stay in touch with Kathy's latest books and projects on her blog at kathyfawcett.com or email the author at kathy@kathyfawcett.com